DELAYED DIAGNOSIS

HAROLD MYERS

Delayed Diagnosis

ISBN
978-1-961250-72-7 (Paperback)
978-1-961250-73-4 (eBook)
978-1-961250-71-0 (Hardcover)

DELAYED DIAGNOSIS

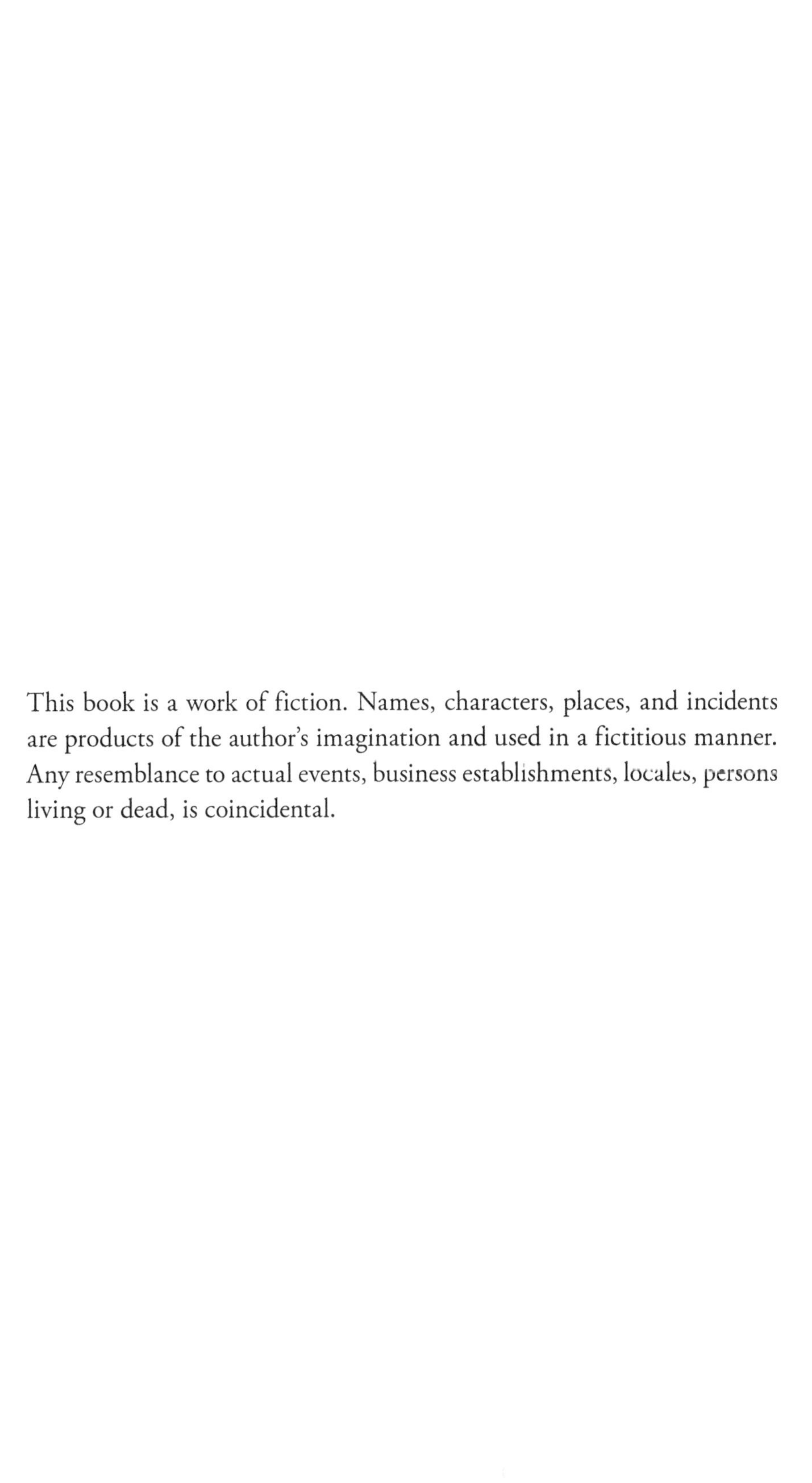

Acknowledgments

To those who have inspired me in my life, encouraged me, shared their thoughts with me and reminded me to be humble, I thank all of you.

To my loving spouse who has provided me an extra push into new directions when writer's block set in and for her patience, understanding and support while this work was in progress.

The physician must ... have two special objects in view regarding disease, namely, to do good or to do no harm.

From the original Hippocratic oath

1
CHAPTER

James Mark Spencer, age sixty-five, awakened from a short nap when he felt the warmth of the sun on his arm as bright sunshine streamed through the windows into the family room of his eldest daughter's home. Once again, he noticed the small brown spot about halfway up the exterior of his right forearm.

The warmth of the sun slightly irritated the spot but more than likely he thought it was just another freckle or one of those brown spots you suddenly seem to develop, as you grow older. Yet, in the last few weeks, James had a feeling the spot appeared to be growing larger; maybe even changing color and it had a very sinister look.

James reminded himself to again voice his concern about the mysterious spot during his next appointment with Doctor Viking, his primary care physician. The doctor was employed by at Coastal Medical Practitioners, also known as CMP and during his last visit to the doctor about four months ago; James had commented to the doctor about the spot and then had shown it to him.

Doctor Viking just smiled at him and very casually told him, 'James, it is just merely a sign of your age. Your six-five and you might as well get used to these age-related things."

James readily accepted this cliché answer from Doctor Viking and since the spot was not really bothering him, he paid no attention to it.

Remembering the doctor's words, James repeated it to himself aloud adding, "Yes, it most likely a part of the aging process or age related as the good doctor would say and I really should not worry myself. In fact, I am not going to worry about it because I am sure there are more concerning ailments, which will grab my attention, as the years pass. I just have to learn to get used to these age-related things."

2
CHAPTER

James then settled back onto the couch and snuggled with the wool throw he used as a blanket. The leather couch was soft and well broken-in and big enough for him to stretch his five feet, nine-inch frame and the ideal place for him to take a short nap. For a few more minutes, he remained on the couch and mentally reviewed his day.

A few hours ago, James and his youngest Granddaughter Susan, had spent part of the morning and early afternoon at the seashore wandering Laguna Beach's cluster of boutiques, art galleries and other tourist shops with their assortment of tee shirts and Made in China products.

Tired of browsing the shops, they stopped for lunch at one of James's favorite spots, The Hotel Saint Clare, right on the edge of the beach with a dining area open to the sunshine and cool ocean breezes. From this spot, diners enjoyed a panoramic view of Catalina Island and the beautiful Southern California coast.

James and his granddaughter took seats next to the railing on the veranda where they could people watch as swimmers and surfers mingled in the water while sunbathers lay on the sand just below where they had chosen to sit.

They studied the menu and soon a waiter appeared to take their food and drink order. It about ten minutes, their food and drinks arrived, and they continued to enjoy the views while having their lunch.

After lunch, they casually strolled along the wooden boardwalk boarding the beach and then found a bench to sit while watching a pickup basketball game. When they got tired of basketball, they moved to another bench further up the beach to watch an exciting two-man team volleyball match.

Time passed quickly and they walked the boardwalk for a few more minutes before deciding to return to Susan's home where James and the couch became reunited.

James and his granddaughter Susan shared several similar traits and the time they spent together was very special to them but to James, it was something he had always dreamed about.

Susan always called him granddaddy. He smiled, knowing he would never tire of hearing that title. Of all the titles James had earned in his life's work, he liked granddaddy the best of all.

3
CHAPTER

James had retired from a key management position at Windstep Electronics approximately a year ago. Windstep had been his employer for over thirty-nine years, when he joined the company directly after serving a three-year stint in the Army. He remained in engineering all thirty-nine years and for the past few years; he served as Vice President of Engineering for the Windstep California organization.

Not bad for a kid from Millinocket Maine, he mused. Now he had retired, there were many times he missed the camaraderie of the morning coffee breaks with old friends and the stress, strains, and excitement of working for a leading-edge high-tech company. However, when his wife Ruth had died very suddenly, he began to question his own potential longevity.

Ruth and he had been thrifty over the years and with the help and financial advice of the company, they had invested wisely. Hence, with the knowledge of being financially independent, James made the decision to retire and to spend his remaining years enjoying his life and large extended family.

It took him time to adjust to his newfound freedom from employment. But quickly he discovered the enjoyment of being in the company of his seven grandchildren. The sons and daughters of his three children, Jill, Pam, and Mason, comprised of four girls and three boys, who all lived within easy driving distance. They were always a close-knit family and now being retired, he had the opportunity to see all of them frequently.

James lived in a medium-sized three-bedroom, one story house, set on a small lot not far from his daughter in Irvine. A typical tract home in a quiet neighborhood with several friendly neighbors. His house and surroundings were well maintained by the homeowners' association and the home had appreciated significantly since purchase.

Originally, Ruth and James had been attracted to the Irvine area, because of its location not far from the ocean and situated not too far away from Los Angeles and San Diego and all the arts and entertainment opportunities these cities had to offer.

He and Ruth had bought the home a few years earlier and expected to spend the rest of their lives together in this house. Unfortunately, when Ruth died, so did the dream.

4
CHAPTER

Since his retirement, James had immersed himself into many projects and the days passed quickly and he had become a creature of habit. He had a set routine he followed almost every day.

He awoke early every morning, and, on the days, he did not go to the community workout room; he started the day by showering and shaving. After dressing, he would walk out through the garage to retrieve the daily Los Angeles Times newspaper found sitting on his driveway, return to the kitchen and pour himself a bowl of Raisin Bran, and added additional raisins and a sliced banana or blueberries and cover it all with skim milk.

Then sitting at a small table in the family room, he would eat his breakfast while continuing to test his knowledge and solve the daily crossword puzzle.

On the days he went to the workout room, he repeated the entire routine after returning from his exercise. It was only after he finished the puzzle or got tired trying to solve the puzzle, would he scan the rest of the paper and then would try quickly to complete his household chores.

Completing the cleanup chores, allowed him the freedom to delve into his other projects, without the guilt feelings of leaving a pile of laundry or a sink cluttered with dirty dishes.

Over the years, Ruth had meticulously established and maintained a large garden, and this became one of James pet projects. He enjoyed tending to the garden full of flowering plants, shrubs, and citrus trees, bordered by rolling mounds of variegated Impatiens. Although he liked the flowers and variety of trees, his real love of gardening sat off on one side in a small, raised bed for growing a reasonable assortment of herbs and his favorite vegetables.

This had become his favorite project as he remembered the good times with Ruth as they bickered over what flowers to plant.

He also enjoyed the freshness of fruits and vegetables you only get when you pick them from your garden and deliver them to your table.

He played bridge at least once weekly at the neighborhood clubhouse and spent other free time either chatting with his neighbors or sitting in front of his home computer accessing the Internet. James had always maintained a full schedule during his work years and retirement did not slow him down. Neither did it diminish James's lifelong intense curiosity for knowledge and learning.

5
CHAPTER

It was while he worked in the garden, a couple of days after the incident at his daughter's house involving the mysterious spot on his arm, when again he could feel the warmth of the sun on his arm. The heat seemed to aggravate the mysterious spot and James had to restrain himself from scratching or rubbing his arm.

He knew he had an appointment to see Doctor Viking next week to receive the results of a recent series of blood tests. Hence, he figured he might as well just wait until the appointment with Doctor Viking.

During this next visit, he assured himself, he would stress the subject with Doctor Viking and explain his growing concern of the nature of the unknown spot. He wanted to know; What do I have? Why does it itch? What is it?

6
CHAPTER

One week later, during another bright and sunny Southern California day, James had an appointment with Doctor Viking for a routine follow-up. The major purpose of the appointment included learning about the results of a comprehensive series of blood tests he had recently taken to provide the doctor a summary of his cholesterol levels and test reports relating to other body parts.

As he drove down Jeffrey Boulevard on his way to the CMP facility, he pasted the plastic lined strawberry fields and the remaining orange groves with trees full of ripe fruit, almost ready for harvesting. Before he realized it, he arrived at the medical plaza on Barranca Parkway.

He quickly found a parking space and as he maneuvered the car into an open space, he again reminded himself to discuss the mysterious spot with Doctor Viking, particularly since the spot, on his forearm, not only appeared to be getting larger, but maybe a color change had occurred.

He got out of his car and walked slowly to front door of the building almost hesitant to enter. He signed the appointment book and discovered the area had a few patients waiting. He found a seat and from a nearby table he picked up a magazine to browse while he waited to see the doctor.

The reception area was painted a soft neutral color, accented with hanging pictures of flowers and coastal scenes. In one corner was a wall mounted magazine rack containing medical brochures highlighting CMP's medical facilities and its broad diagnostic capabilities.

James had only been seated a few moments when the receptionist called his name. She reminded him of his responsibility for a ten-dollar copayment.

As part of his retirement package, James received HMO coverage and he had selected CMP because of its medical reputation and the proximity of his home to their medical offices.

Within a few minutes, a nurse called his name and escorted him into an examination area. She checked and recorded his weight and then lightly stuck a thermometer in his ear to measure his current body temperature.

When she was finished, she directed him to a small examining room where she asked him a few questions regarding his general health and the purpose of his visit. She then proceeded to take his blood pressure while asking him about existing medications. As she continued to perform the various procedures, she recorded all the information into his chart.

When she had completed all the baseline work, she started to retreat out of the room but turned to inform him, "Make yourself comfortable Mr. Spencer, the doctor will be with you in a few minutes."

Being an engineer, James found these rooms fascinating with their wide variety of medical devices and instruments. There were instruments for checking ears, blood pressure, and of course, the ever-present examination table, with its' white paper cover. On one wall, a large rack had been mounted and filled with a supply of pamphlets on smoking, TB, weight loss, pregnancy, hypertension, and cholesterol; all published by drug companies, vying for the patient's and doctor's attention. On the opposite wall was a large picture showing the various arteries and major organs of the body.

James then noticed a pamphlet describing the symptoms of a heart attack and selected it to read. He had not finished reading the first page when Doctor Viking entered the room.

Doctor Viking never just walked into the room; he bounced into the room on his Air Jordan sneakers, accented with expensive stone washed jeans. His long straight blond hair spilled over onto the collar of the white starched lab coat he wore with the CMP logo. He had a small diamond in his left ear lobe and obviously was a doctor of the MTV generation. The only real distinguishing feature, which James's thought made him look like a doctor, was the white lab coat and the stethoscope draped around his neck.

"James, how are you? You're looking great, your chart says you're great, and from the results of all your blood tests, you are a picture of good health.

Your cholesterol is still a little higher than I like but you stick to your low-fat diet and using your meds and you will continue to make progress. You should also continue to keep up your exercise program and I assure you; you'll be fine. Now, is anything else bothering you before I send you home?"

James answered in a rather meek voice. "Well, Doctor Viking, I still have this spot on my right forearm which appears to be growing larger and darker. It also becomes irritated at times; usually itchier than irritated. Remember, you checked this spot, the last time I came here in May?"

Doctor Viking carefully lifted James's arm and took a quick look. "Let me see. Ah yes, another one of your age spots and more than likely irritated by too much sun.

Nothing you should be too concerned about. I'll leave a prescription for you at the reception desk for a Cortisone based ointment. Use the ointment liberally twice daily and stay out of the sun for a while or at least, keep your arms covered. Use some good sunscreen of SPF 30 or greater, particularly when you are working in your garden or walking in the sun. Let me know how it's going in a couple of weeks. Good seeing you again and James, you can take the pamphlet with you."

He was out the door, almost as fast as he came in; nothing unusual James reminded himself, he had never spent more than five minutes with Doctor Viking, in all the time he had been a patient of CMP. Obviously, he is paid like a piece-part worker on CMP's production line. Welcome to the HMO factory of modern medicine thought James.

He left the room and headed towards the reception desk to retrieve his prescription. The receptionist had his prescription ready for him and after receiving his prescription; he returned to his car and drove to a nearby drug store to have the prescription filled, before continuing the ride home.

He was happy he had spoken to the doctor about his spot concern, but he had not given any further thought about the possible severity of the spot, nor the itchiness, the periodic irritation, and the possible color change. He had accepted Doctor Vikings' diagnosis and convinced himself, if I start using the medicine today, soon the spot will disappear almost as quickly as it had arrived.

7 CHAPTER

Lionel Viking, MD, grew up in the City of Compton, California a few miles southwest of Los Angeles. It was one of the oldest cities in Los Angeles County but at his young age, it did not mean anything to Lionel. He didn't remember too much about his early childhood. Perhaps if he did remember, he certainly did not want to be reminded of it.

As a youngster, he lived in a very small two-bedroom apartment with his mother. Lionel didn't know his father because he had no father who lived with him. He also had no awareness of his mother, Mary Beth Viking, living off the system collecting welfare and food stamps during his early years.

The HUD office in Compton, which had provided her with a subsidized apartment, knew her very well. She always complained about the apartment she shared with Lionel as it was either too small, too noisy or it had bad neighbors. The HUD personnel were kind enough not to remind her, she didn't pay rent.

She had very few skills and didn't even try to work because she knew the system well enough to get whatever the city, state or federal government gave away. It did not bother her one bit and just because she was a welfare mom, she still had all the rights of others and hey, she felt if she was smart enough to get all the freebies, she deserved them.

Just like James Spencer, Mary Beth also had a daily regimen but unlike James, hers included sleeping in until midmorning and when she finely decided to get up, she would call her friends and find out which food pantries had the day's best giveaways. She would then grab Lionel, stuff him into an old beat-up stroller she had been given by a thrift store and they would make their way through the city streets of Compton to the food pantry of the day.

After gathering up all her food pantry and thrift store articles for the day, she would then head back to the apartment, pushing young Lionel in the beat-up stroller, to waste the rest of the day.

Later, as the sun began to set, she would feed Lionel and put him to bed and then sit and wait for Lionel to fall asleep. Once she knew he was asleep, she would then take her pocketbook and leave for her favorite hangout, Cooks Bar & Grill over on Fourth Street, just a couple blocks away.

At Cook's she knew most of the regulars and many of them also worked the system just like Mary Beth. Besides the low-cost beer and nightly companionship, Cooks offered another benefit; for the regulars they traded food stamps for beer.

The City of Compton demographics would categorize itself as a multiracial city but composed of a limited number of Anglos and Asians. The largest share of the population was African Americans, who had migrated from the South and Hispanics legal and illegal, who probably made their way across the Arizona border or into San Diego by way of Tijuana.

Most of them had settled in Compton mainly to be among the people they knew best, the proximity to Los Angeles, where there were jobs and the advantage of lower cost housing in the City of Compton.

The regulars at Cooks Bar & Grill were a microcosm of the city itself. The popular bar became the favorite for many African Americans and Hispanics and for whatever reason; Lionel's mother had an attraction for both ethnicities.

Hence, young Lionel often discovered either one color or another sleeping in his mother's bed on any given morning. He never liked any of them and they rarely even acknowledged he existed. He did however resent when they became abusive to his mother, but she shrugged it off as being the normal way those types of macho men treat their women. Lionel never accepted it, but it did not stop Mary Beth from going to Cooks nightly.

8
CHAPTER

When he reached school age, Lionel attended neighborhood schools and although a bright student, he didn't fit into the mold of many of his classmates. He didn't care for sports; he could not speak the street lingo of the African Americans and he did not want to learn Spanish. He became the square block trying to fit into the round circle.

He did however realize, at an early age, he wanted to become somebody important. Like most kids, he equated important people to wealth.

He learned how important people dressed and how they acted and where they lived and what model cars they drove. He digested all of this while he was young and he knew, someday people would see him as an important person. For Lionel, being an important person became his primary goal and focus.

When he finally reached high school, he became a very serious student. He strove to always excel in every class he attended and participated in school activities, which focused on intellect. The Science and Debate Clubs were among his favorites, and he became proficiently articulate.

In his third year of high school, He ran for class president and got easily elected. Yet, with all his scholastic success, he had a very limited number of friends, did not date and he purposely avoided any relationship with his African American or Hispanic classmates regardless of their intellect.

Meanwhile, he and his mother were like ships passing in the night. No affection existed between her, and Lionel and she paid little to no attention to him. He learned to fend for himself for meals, laundry, and anything else he may have required. Mary Beth made no effort to alter any of her usual habits and she rarely spoke to her son and Lionel did his best to avoid her. During his teen years, he did learn about his mother exploiting the welfare system and he resented his mother because of her actions and lack of ambition. They were two people living together, who had grown very far apart.

As he got older, he knew he had grown beyond her, and he never expected her to change. She would always be the person she had been since he was a young child. His focus remained on achieving success and to becoming someone important. Whereas she was content on being the person she always had been.

He openly confided with his few close school friends, "The City of Compton and his mother would never see him again, once he graduated high school."

9
CHAPTER

Lionel continued to excel scholastically in his last two years of high school and made the decision, he wanted to become a doctor. He knew it represented the road towards importance and the ticket out of Compton.

Because of his excellent grades and his high SAT scores he received scholarships and acceptance to attend UCLA and he began his first semester in the fall after graduation from high school. Moving into school housing, he found a part time job in clothing store and true to his promise, he never again returned to Compton or talked to his mother.

The years passed quickly, and he did very well in his pre-med undergraduate studies and got accepted to attend medical school within the same university. Four years later, he graduated at about the top of his class and accepted a two-year residency at the Los Angeles County Hospital.

Based upon his previous non-association with minorities while in high school, it appeared strange he had accepted a residency at the county hospital because it had a patient population composed heavily of African American, and Hispanic patients.

After being there for a short time, Lionel began to openly expose his dislike for either ethnicity to other residents or staff members. He often referred to these people as "freeloaders" or those "no pay bums" and he said, "if it were left to me, I would kick them in the ass and toss them out onto the street."

His superiors heard of his comments from other hospital staff and noted his time spent with any patient of color was short and non-clinical. Hence, in a short time, the Director of Residency, Doctor Tobias, scheduled a meeting with Lionel and his immediate supervisor to discuss his antisocial behavior towards minority patients.

When it came time for the meeting, Lionel and his supervisor entered the Director's office and Doctor Tobias directed Lionel to a chair directly in front of his desk.

He started his talk as follows: "Mr. Viking, I want you to understand the seriousness of this meeting. You are here today because of your unacceptable behavior, as a person and as a medical professional, directed towards minorities. This hospital has strict rules and procedures how we treat all patients regardless of race, color or religion and you sir are not adhering to any of our standards," said, Doctor Tobias.

"You have been accepted here to become a doctor, but you are failing the test. If you still have ambitions of ever becoming a doctor, then you must learn to adhere to the standards set by this hospital and your peer doctors.

Begin treating every patient as if they were your mother. As Director of Residency at this hospital, I expect you to show all patients respect and provide them with an accurate clear diagnosis or prognosis. You must learn to listen to their troubles and then use the knowledge and skills you possess to administer to them and heal them."

"Do you fully understand what I have said and the consequences of your not adhering to the established rules and procedures?"

Lionel had listened intently to the Director before replying. "Sir, I do understand, and I am sorry for my previous actions and will not repeat them again. I do want to become a doctor and I will not disappoint you or other members of this hospital. I promise, I will immediately amend my behavior and I will treat all patients fairly and to the best of my ability. Again sir, please accept my apology."

What he didn't tell Doctor Tobias, he was treating them like his mother, who he disliked as much as he did African Americans and Hispanics.

"I accept your apology and expect you perform as you have promised me, I also expect you to uphold the standards of this hospital now and wherever your future assignments may take you." said Doctor Tobias.

10 CHAPTER

After the meeting with Doctor Tobias, Lionel kept his promise and became a poster boy for race relations at the hospital. At least on the surface for others to see, but when by himself, he dreamed of the day he would finish residency so he could then decide for himself what kind of people he would treat and the rest of those with medical needs could go elsewhere.

He maintained his good boy behavior for the remaining time he needed to complete his residency. He had no further blemishes on his record and finished his residency training exactly on time.

Upon completion of training, he received his certifications and licenses to practice medicine in the State of California. He had no further ambitions to continue into a specialty field and when CMP offered him a position as a Primary Care Doctor, he readily accepted.

He would have preferred to have entered private practice, but he did not have any access to money to open an office or even the funds needed for his own support.

CMP assigned him to the West, LA office as a new Primary Care Doctor and within a few weeks at this location he again began to randomly discriminate against minorities but unlike his previous actions during his residency, at CMP he made it a point of being very careful not to openly demonstrate his dislikes nor orally state his bigoted hatred of minorities.

He accomplished this by sugarcoating his presentations to minority patients as an attempt to gain their confidence. But then he would give them only limited examinations and simplified diagnoses.

He became a master of manipulation by treating minority patients quickly and then would provide them stories of a non-life-threatening condition, which he could then offer as a diagnosis they could readily accept as fact.

He gave them a misdiagnosis and he prided himself on his intellect and their easy acceptance of his comments. He knew he could rely on the accepted patient/physician trust factor to sell his lies.

However, in the seventh month of his employment, his luck finally ran out and his bad behavior surfaced and came to the attention of CMP management.

He had assured an elderly Asian woman, who had complained of chest pains to Doctor Viking during a routine appointment, it was only a case of mild acid reflux. A few days later, the woman suffered a mild heart attack.

The Cardiologist at the admitting hospital where the paramedics brought the women had asked for a copy of the patient's medical history. The doctor could not believe what he read from her record. It clearly showed; she had complained of her condition to Doctor Viking one week before experiencing her heart attack.

The Cardiologist later submitted his findings to his chief of staff who forwarded the compliant to higher-level management.

CMP management reviewed the sequence of events and became convinced a young doctor had just made a rookie mistake. The fact of the woman being a minority never entered into the management review. The corporation quickly and quietly settled with the patient and per corporate policy, transferred Doctor Viking to the CMP Irvine offices. His personnel record contained only a minor comment about the mistake by Doctor Viking and the subsequent action taken by CMP.

The way Lionel thought, he had a right to his personal likes and dislikes, and it didn't really bother him to be reprimanded and transferred by CPM.

11 CHAPTER

James continued his usual routine for the next few days after his visit to Doctor Viking and used the prescribed medication as directed. He made sure he applied the ointment to the spot on his arm twice daily and he wore long sleeve shirts to avoid exposure to the sun. In addition, he applied liberal amounts of sunscreen whenever he went outside to work in his garden and whenever he walked to the workout room or to his weekly bridge game at the clubhouse.

He followed Doctor Viking's directions word for word, and he assumed, based on everything he did, the medication would be helpful in eliminating the spot and it would soon go disappear.

After the eighth day of treatment, James began to have serious doubts and concerns about the effectiveness of the medicine he faithfully applied to his arm. By the tenth day he knew the treatments had shown no visible indication of any improvement or any healing and yet, the irritation and itching became a frequent daily occurrence.

When he showered; it appeared the spot quickly became sensitive to the warmth of the water, and he finally accepted the fact the medication proved to be ineffective in healing or eliminating the spot. James decided to stop using the ointment immediately and to quickly obtain another appointment to review the situation with the doctor.

He telephoned the offices of CMP and the earliest he would be able to have an appointment with Doctor Viking, would be in four days.

While waiting for his appointment day to arrive, James had difficulty concentrating on even the easiest task. He found it difficult to look at the spot and when he did, he knew the color had slightly changed and the spot had grown to be larger, rising above his skin. In addition, it had become more painful and continued to be irritated.

His sleeping became very fitful and uncomfortable for him as pain emanating from the spot would awaken him if he moved in the wrong direction during the night.

When the day for his appointment arrived, James seemed relieved hoping this visit would end his nightmare over the mysterious spot.

He arrived at CMP's offices a few minutes before his scheduled visit, paid his ten-dollar copayment, found a comfortable chair, and picked up a magazine while waiting admission to the examination area.

Within ten minutes, a nurse came into the reception area and called his name, and he followed the nurse into the examination area. She asked the usual questions and recorded data about his current vitals. She then escorted him to one of the small examination rooms and advised him the doctor would be with him shortly. She quietly left the room closing the door behind her.

While he waited for Doctor Viking, James again selected the pamphlet on heart attacks. This time he had read about three pages when the door to the room opened and to his surprise, in walked a stranger.

"Hello Mr. Spencer, I'm Doctor Mancetti."

"Hello Doctor. Glad to meet you but I expected to see Doctor Viking today?"

"Doctor Viking has been recently assigned to our Fountain Valley Office and I am replacing Doctor Viking for all his patients."

"I will now serve as your primary care physician for the immediate future. Now, before I continue any further, I need about another five minutes to review your chart and history. I apologize for the wait, but I promise you, I won't be more than five minutes. You relax and continue your reading of the pamphlet and I'll be right back." After completing his opening remarks, Doctor Mancetti left the room.

Well, thought James, at least he looks and acts like a doctor, and he has all the appearances and characteristics James had always expected of a doctor. Conservatively dressed and approximately six feet tall, he wore a white shirt and tie under his CMP starched lab coat and around his neck hung the usual stethoscope. His hair had begun to gray at the temples, which provided James a clue of his age, early forties.

The doctor had just turned forty-two and had been a doctor for over fifteen years, recently joining CMP as a Senior Staff Physician.

Before James could do any further speculation, Doctor Mancetti reentered the room carrying James' chart and medical history, exactly four minutes after he had left.

Doctor Mancetti began to speak as he walked through the door. "Sorry for the slight delay, Mr. Spencer, but someone tried to corral me in the corridor. They will have to wait until we are finished. I have read your chart and some of your history and I understand you came here today because of a lingering skin problem. Please tell me a little more about it; where it is located; when did you first notice it; does it hurt, etc.?"

James thought for a long moment, slightly raised his sleeve, and pointed to the spot and then began to answer the doctor's question. "This spot has been on my right arm for more than six months now, but I am not exactly sure when I first noticed it. I have pointed it out to Doctor Viking in a couple of previous examinations around last April or May. Most recently, maybe two weeks ago, Doctor Viking looked at it again and he prescribed a Cortisone based ointment mainly to reduce the itching and he advised me to liberally use sunscreen and limit my exposure to the sun.

I have followed his directions including applying the application of the ointment twice daily for almost two weeks. Yet the spot is still there, and I sense, it has been increasing in size and appears to be changing color. At times it does become rather painful, very itchy, and irritated. It even wakes me at night when I turn on my right side."

While he had been speaking, James had continued to roll up his sleeve to better expose the small spot located on the exterior of his forearm, just below his elbow. It was about a quarter of an inch in diameter at its widest point, nodular and slightly elevated above the skin with a very irregular shape, like scalloping on the edge of a leave. It had a light and dark brownish coloration accented with two or more visible black spots sitting amongst the brown background.

Doctor Mancetti immediately recognized the seriousness of the growth but kept it to himself, as he did not want to upset the patient. To the doctor, it appeared as a very ominous looking growth because of the size and coloring.

"What do you mean by irritated, James? Can you further describe it to me?"

"It gets itchy." James felt tense but continued to speak. "It also feels sore at times, particularly when the shower water hits it or even when I am in the sun. I suppose the heat from either the shower or the sun irritates it and makes it itchy. Yet still, my concern now and has been, whatever it may be, it doesn't seem to be going away and this observation makes it real scary for me."

Unknowingly, James had lowered his voice and Doctor Mancetti noted James's uncertainty about speaking about his problem; almost, as if apologizing or being too embarrassed to speak about it.

"Honestly, Doctor, I am sort of glad and relieved I am not seeing Doctor Viking and I am pleased I can now get an additional opinion" said James softly.

"Mr. Spencer, you don't have apologize or feel embarrassed about wanting a second opinion. If you don't understand something, then it is reasonable for you to ask.

As doctors, we want you to feel confident about your care. I appreciate your concern, for your wellbeing, and quite frankly, I wish more patients would speak up. Thank you for having provided me a good clear explanation of how it affects you."

"Now, let me look at your arm so I can have the opportunity to provide you a possible diagnosis. Please take a seat over here by this table. I would like to look at the area a little closer, but I want to look under much more favorable lighting."

The doctor also took a seat next to the metal table and then Doctor Mancetti carefully took James' arm in his hand and rested it on a padded portion of the table, which also held several packaged surgical instruments. Doctor Mancetti shined the light of a small high intensity lamp directly onto the area of the forearm. Immediately the lamp highlighted the spot in a very similar fashion to when the sun had highlighted it for James while he lay on the couch at his daughter's home. Doctor Mancetti moved the skin gently back and forth between his fingers and studied the spot for about 30 seconds using a small magnifying glass, before he began speaking again.

"Mr. Spencer, you were correct in being concerned and I am also concerned but I am not fully certain as to the exact diagnosis. It would be much better for you if a specialist provided a diagnosis and therefore, I recommend you be referred to our staff dermatologist, Doctor Stuart. I am sure, I can arrange for you to see him later this week or at the very latest, early next week. In the meantime, if you have not stopped using the prescribed ointment, please do so now, but do continue to use sunscreen and try to avoid excessive exposure to the sun."

"Doctor Stuart will provide me information regarding his findings, and I will personally provide the results to you.

Now Mr. Spencer, it was a pleasure to meet you and if you wait in the reception area for a few minutes, I will have Mary, our receptionist, try to contact Doctor Stuart. Mary will provide you details regarding the appointment along with directions to Doctor Stuart's office.

Whenever the results become available, I promise you, we will call you. In the meantime, if you have any questions, call me. I always return my calls, usually, early in the morning."

12
CHAPTER

After his conversation and further examination of James, Doctor Mancetti left the examination room and immediately went to his office. On the way, he stopped at the reception desk and spoke to the receptionist.

"Mary, please get me Doctor Stuart, our resident dermatologist, on the phone, and when you make contact, please transfer the call into my office. If he is not there, I'll speak to whomever might be covering for him."

Doctor Mancetti turned around and quickly left for his office to await the call. Mary noted from both his verbal and physical demeanor, a very visible unhappy doctor.

In less than a minute, Mary had reached Doctor Stuart and had transferred the call into Doctor Mancetti's office.

"Doctor Stuart, Doctor Mancetti of the Irvine facility. Please call me Bob. I'm relatively new here; I understand you treat a number our patients with skin issues?"

"Pleasure to meet you. Doctor, call me Peter. Yes, we do treat a few your patients; now how can I assist you?"

"Peter, we have a sixty-five-year-old male, relatively healthy in all respects, but with a suspicious growth on the

exterior of his right forearm; irregular in shape, elevated and slightly discolored. He complains of both irritation and tenderness. There also is a strong possibility of the growth growing during the last few weeks in the affected area. I have carefully examined the area and I am quite frankly very concerned for the patient. I would hope you could arrange to see him in the next day or two, as I believe he needs a specialist to see him very soon. If you could check on an appointment day and time, I will arrange to have his chart faxed to you immediately."

"Sounds ominous. Any guess at a diagnosis doctor?" asked Doctor Stuart.

Doctor Mancetti quickly replied. "I do Peter, but it's the reason I called you; I value the opinion of a specialist and I would prefer, based upon experience, not to make any wild guesses. However, I do have an opinion and will answer your question after you provide the diagnosis.

I also believe, based upon what I have read from the patient's chart, he should have been referred to a dermatologist, at least two or three months ago and maybe even sooner." Doctor Mancetti hesitated for a long moment, and then added rather solemnly; "Frankly, regarding my diagnosis, I do hope, I am wrong."

"Considering your description and the circumstances, I'm sure we can always accommodate another patient tomorrow and Bob from the tone of your voice, I also hope you are wrong."

"Thanks, Peter. Let me transfer you back to Mary and she will convey the appointment information to the patient and directions to your office. She also will fax his chart over to you very soon. Again, thanks for the help and I will stay in contact with you regarding this patient."

Within a short time after talking to Doctor Mancetti and his receptionist, Doctor Stuart was deeply engrossed in reading James's medical file he had received by way of fax from the Irvine office of CMP. He was puzzled by the number of notations in the records referring to a potential skin condition, including a scribbled comment with the word skin cancer, followed by a question mark.

Doctor Mancetti had performed a very thorough examination of the area under consideration including detailed descriptions of size and coloration. It was obvious to Doctor Stuart, Doctor Mancetti either suspected or knew outright that James's problem went well beyond a simple skin disorder or an age-related spot.

Doctor Mancetti certainly had reason in being concerned, thought Doctor Stuart and once he had read the chart, he also felt Mr. James Spencer should have been examined by someone with a lot more intelligence more than six months ago.

He sure did not relish seeing this patient tomorrow and with the thought still on his mind, he paper clipped the file together and added a Post-it Note to the top page. It simply said, "create a file for James Mark Spencer" and he angrily tossed it into his out-basket.

Meanwhile, back at Irvine's CMP offices, the receptionist had given James the appointment information and the driving directions to reach Doctor Stuarts office.

After receiving the information, He left the medical offices and returned to his car where he sat for a long time inundated with thoughts of possible dire medical outcomes after his meeting with Doctor Mancetti.

The doctor had spent much more time with him then Doctor Viking ever had ever done but his mind went into overdrive with images of various skin ailments, both real and imagined. He felt his quality of life being threatened and he felt defenseless against this strange and eerie spot.

Slowly, James drives home. He liked Doctor Mancetti, but he could not help but to sense from the doctor's first look, his body language and from the tone of his voice, there was a lot more concern about a serious problem than the doctor was willing to share with him at this time.

13
CHAPTER

By the time James arrived home, he had ruled out most of the deadly thoughts swirling in his mind. He settled on the original diagnosis of age spots and excessive sensitivity to the sun, the phrases used by Doctor Viking, as being the causes of the mysterious brown spot on his arm. Subconsciously, he did this mainly to ease his anxiety and perhaps to mentally escape from the reality of his situation.

He had just opened his front door when he heard the telephone ringing in the family room. Closing the door and running quickly from the front of the house to the family room, he reached for the telephone and upon saying hello, heard his brother Bob calling from Boston, just wanting to say hello and to chat.

"Hi Bob, what's up and how's the family?"

"Everyone is fine, James. You sound like you have been out running again or do you have breathing difficulties?"

"No, nothing to do with my breathing. I just walked in the door from a visit with my doctor and I had to run from the front door to the family room to answer the telephone."

"You seem to have had many doctor visits lately. Do you have some medical issues you have not confided to anyone?" asked Bob.

James tried his best to put a positive spin on his concerns. "Well, maybe, but I am not real certain. So up to now, I haven't said anything to anybody.

I do have a spot on my arm, which has been there for a while and it looks like a big freckle, except its ugly, sort of lumpy and it bothers me every now and then. My doctor appeared to be a little concerned and has referred me to a dermatologist and I have an appointment with the doctor tomorrow morning."

"It's probably nothing, but just to be on the safe side, I'm going to have the specialist look at it and let him give me the diagnosis."

"It sounds to me like it is a little more serious than you are willing to acknowledge. How long have you suspected it might be a problem, James?"

"Realistically, only recently. Honestly, I have known about it for four or five months now and I did discuss it with my old primary care doctor on more than one occasion, but he just felt it had to do with my age. You know those age-related brown spots."

"Four or five months! James, you do have medical coverage, don't you?"

"Yes," said James sheepishly.

"Then, why the procrastination? Since you were a kid, you have a consistent history of trying to avoid seeing doctors. Hell, you have plenty of money and besides, medical benefits certainly are part of your retirement package. What's the problem? You earned it and paid for it, didn't you? So, use it."

"Thanks for the pep talk, Bob. I'm doing it. It's just, well, up till now, I didn't see it as a problem. It is only in the last few weeks I started to become concerned." James suddenly changed the subject.

"Now enough about me, I will be fine. How about you and the family? What about Roberta and the new baby? You and Marge are a few grandchildren ahead of me. I am jealous and I'll have to tell my kids to play catch-up."

"The children are all fine, James and besides, my kids are a few years older than yours. I suggest you let your kids decide if they want more children. Tell all of them I said hello and please call me after you get the results from your dermatology visit. I am concerned with what you told me."

"Thanks for the call, Bob; I do appreciate your interest and concern. I'll keep you informed, but it's probably nothing but my wild imagination. Give Marge a hug for me. Bye now."

James placed the receiver back into the telephone cradle and slowly walked into the kitchen to prepare dinner.

Searching the refrigerator, he found some two-day-old, leftover Chinese food, which he plopped onto a plate, covered it with a paper towel and heated it in the microwave oven. Three minutes later, he began eating the concoction, which disappeared in another two minutes, and he quickly gulped a glass of water. After finishing his hastily prepared dinner, he dropped the dirty plate into the sink and wandered into the family room.

He tried to get comfortable on another one of his favorite spots for napping, the old leather couch in the family room. He clicked on the television, rapidly switching channels, until he finally selected a channel he liked and began watching an old rerun of the Honeymooners.

Settling himself on the couch, he had problems concentrating as his mind continued to wonder about tomorrow's appointment with the dermatologist and the probable results. For some reason, unbeknownst to him, he felt a slight queasiness in his stomach unrelated to his hastily prepared dinner. Fortunately, within a few minutes he fell asleep, while on television, Ralph was threatening to send Alice to the moon.

He woke around midnight and finding himself still on the couch, he slowly made his way into the bedroom.

Undressing in the dimly lit room, he stared at the spot on his arm. It was very visible, even in the dimly lit room and stood out on his arm like a lone star in the sky against a black background. Yet again he convinced himself it was nothing to get alarmed about and besides, it was up to the doctor to determine if a problem existed.

With this last thought, he got into bed, fluffed his pillow, shut the light and without any further negative thoughts, he went back to sleep.

14 CHAPTER

James awoke at his usual early time of five-thirty am, staggered into the bathroom, splashed some water on his face to complete his wake up and then quickly dressed in sweatpants and a fleece top. He realized, he had about eight hours of time to use up before the time of his scheduled appointment with the dermatologist. He might as well spend the time following his regular routine, which he hoped would allow the time to pass quicker.

He left his home to walk the short distance to the workout room located in the community clubhouse about one block away. He decided a brisk walk would do him good and hopefully relieve some of the tension he felt, almost immediately after he awoke. When he entered the clubhouse workout room, he made his way to an unused treadmill, climbed aboard, and set the speed for a brisk 4.2 miles per hour pace with a slight incline.

He spent the next thirty-five minutes on the treadmill working up a sweat and working off some calories and stress. Upon completion, he normally would have gone on to lift some free weights but today he passed on doing strength training and left the clubhouse and slowly walked home to shower, read the paper, and eat his breakfast.

As he stood under the warm shower, he stared at the spot on his forearm and his brow wrinkled in concern. He said to himself, “I should probably refer to the spot as a growth as Doctor referred to it.

The force and heat of the water made the growth sensitive to the touch and itchy and James had to restrain from scratching the area. He quickly finished showering, dried himself, shaved, put on a bathrobe, and went looking for his newspaper in the driveway.

With the paper, he returned to the kitchen to prepare his usual breakfast and while still eating, he began to do the crossword puzzle. Within a few minutes, he gave up trying to do the puzzle realizing he could not concentrate on anything except the upcoming appointment and yet, his appointment with Doctor Stuart was not until two p.m., still some six or seven hours away.

He knew the stress of this ordeal was beginning to trouble him, but he knew from the time he woke up this morning, this would not be an easy day for him. He also knew it had been a troublesome month.

He attempted to spend the rest of the morning doing odds and ends around the house but with his depressed feeling combined with a sense of doom, he accomplished very little. Stress had taken control of his every movement and thought and none of the thoughts were positive.

Finally, around twelve thirty, he dressed and got ready for his appointment with Doctor Stuart. The doctor's office was only about a twenty-minute drive away, but he felt perhaps by getting there early, maybe he would reduce some of the stress he felt along with the cloud of uncertainty, which he now admitted to himself, plagued him from the time he had been examined by Doctor Mancetti.

The drive to the Doctor Stuart's office did not take very long and soon he found himself, sitting in the waiting room, waiting his turn to meet the doctor. Oblivious to his surroundings and too nervous to read a magazine, he could not concentrate on anything but thoughts of doom, which continued to swirl in his mind.

Meanwhile, Doctor Stuart had returned from lunch and read a note from his nurse stating James had arrived early for his appointment.

He called her and said, "Betty, please give me a few more minutes before you get Mr. Spencer and then do the normal vitals and let me know of his demeanor. When you are finished with the vitals, please take him to room two and ensure we have everything ready to do a biopsy."

Since James had arrived so very early, he had to wait twenty-seven minutes before the nurse called his name and she took him to the general examination area to perform the usual nurse chores. She then took him to another smaller examination room to wait for Doctor Stuart. She asked him a few more questions and advised him the doctor would be in to see him in a few minutes.

After the nurse left the room, James sat in the closest chair but did not reach for any of the many pamphlets resting in the rack on the wall. Concerned about his fate and wondering about his destiny occupied his thoughts.

Meanwhile, sitting in his office, Doctor Stuart picked up James's file and began reading it again. Betty briefly appeared in his office to advise him of her observations of James.

"Overall, most of his vital readings match closely with prior test results. Blood pressure somewhat elevated but not so bad and it should be expected considering the reason for the visit. There is no doubt; we have a very nervous patient and quite possibly despondent," said Betty.

Doctor Stuart thanked Betty and continued sitting at his desk feeling he knew the outcome of this diagnosis long before he would ever see the patient.

Not a very good feeling he thought, not a good feeling for any doctor and it will not be good news for the patient.

15
CHAPTER

With a bit of reluctance and trepidation, Doctor Stuart rose from his chair and slowly walked to room two; opened the door and slowly entered.

"Mr. Spencer, I'm Doctor Stuart and assisting me today will be my nurse assistant, Betty. "How are you feeling today?"

Before James could answer, Doctor Stuart immediately confirmed Betty's comments and recognized a very depressed patient.

"I'm fine, Doctor except for some nervousness about this spot," said James.

Trying to be upbeat and positive, Doctor Stuart said rather casually "Well, I have read your chart and understand the reason for your being here today. Before we start, I have a couple of questions to ask you."

"Did doctor Viking ever suggest for you to see a dermatologist?"

James looked surprised at the question and just nodded his head indicating a no answer.

"Did you ever consider seeking an opinion from a dermatologist?"

Again, James just nodded his head suggesting another no answer.

"Thanks James," said Doctor Stuart.

"We might as well get on with the examination because neither one of us can make any judgments about a diagnosis without first doing an examination."

"Mr. Spencer lets you and I move over to the table by the wall. Please sit here and I want you to rest your arm on this pad to allow me to have a clear view of the spot in question. I am going to dim the overhead lights slightly now and turn on this high intensity lamp to obtain a clearer view of the affected area. Are you comfortable?"

"Yes," James said but his stress level was obvious.

"Can I give you some medication to reduce your anxiety?"

"I'll be fine doctor. Let's just proceed and I will get through it okay."

After James rejection of medication, Doctor Stuart began the procedure by peering through magnifying glasses he had put on to study the growth on James' arm, now being illuminated by the lamp on the table. After studying the growth for a few minutes including checking the size and color of the spot, Doctor Stuart spoke.

"Mr. Spencer, what I am looking at is a cancerous growth and now it becomes necessary I perform a biopsy of the growth so I can learn more about it from a detailed lab analysis. The surgery will only involve a very small incision on a section of your arm, and it will not be painful as I will apply some deadening medication to the affected area before attempting a biopsy. I also will be removing the entire growth and in addition, I will be removing a small portion of the skin surrounding the suspected growth."

"I want you to understand, I am performing a fairly common procedure and the biopsy specimen together with a culture will later get analyzed for various types of cancer. In addition, a sample of the biopsy specimen will be studied to determine the make-up and structure of the cells in the sample. I know I have given you much information to digest and if you have any questions at any time, please do not be afraid to ask. Lastly, Mr. Spencer are you comfortable enough for us to begin?" asked Doctor Stuart?

"Are you saying I have cancer, doctor?

"Not yet, but from my experience I know most growths of this type are cancerous and some are more.

serious than others. What type of cancer? I don't know until we have completed a biopsy and have seen the results of the completed lab analysis on the removed specimen."

James shuddered when he heard the word cancer but agreed to continue with the procedure knowing it would provide further details and a probable diagnosis of the condition, which had been troubling him for some time. He wanted to know, but again he felt the uneasiness in his stomach particularly when he heard the word cancer spoken by Doctor Stuart. He knew, a conclusion would soon be known but this did not stop him from feeling the stress begin to build and it began to permeate his entire body. His only temporary distraction would be Doctor Stuart cutting into his arm.

"Mr. Spencer, I know this is stressful for you; so, can I give you a mild sedative to relax you a bit?"

"No thank you, Doctor. Give me a moment to steady myself. I am just nervous and please call me James."

"You do not have to apologize, James. You have gone through a lot lately and I understand your nervousness is based upon your concerns and fears. I can also assure you; this is entirely normal for all patients having to go through this procedure. Let's first really determine a lot more about the growth on your arm."

After trying to calm James, Doctor Stuart asked Betty for several instruments, which she retrieved from a sterile container.

Doctor Stuart could still sense James' apprehension. He advised James he had to cleanse the area where he would perform the biopsy first and then would deaden the area so James would not sense any pain.

He started the procedure by cleaning a small area of about three quarters of an inch around the growth in which he would perform the biopsy while being very careful not to apply excessive pressure to the growth. Then, he sprayed an anesthetic solution on James' arm to numb the entire area and lastly, he carefully applied another anesthetic solution into the area by way of a syringe.

James could feel the area become warm and then numb almost instantly and to some measure, it relaxed him a little and his interest shifted to the procedure about to be performed by the doctor.

Doctor Stuart waited about two minutes for the anesthetic solution to fully take effect before he began the biopsy surgical process to remove the entire growth. He skillfully and carefully cut around the growth using a small but obviously sharp scalpel. He cut about one quarter inch below the skin surface to remove as much of the growth as he could see through the magnifying glasses, he had put on earlier when he started the procedure. He then used small sterile tweezers to remove the surgical scrapings and placed them into a Petri Dish previously labeled with the patient's name and date. When he had completed the procedure, he replaced the cover to the dish and set it aside.

"James, I think I have removed the major portion of the growth. I am now going to cover it with a bandage, and I want you to leave the bandage on for the rest of today and replace it tomorrow. After the second day, you can wash it with warm water by gently dabbing the water onto the sore. Replace the bandage daily for at least six days. You may have some soreness on your arm for the next one or two days and if the discomfort troubles you, take a couple of Tylenol."

"We will provide you with written instructions on what you must do over the next week or so."

"The laboratory pathology of the removed specimen will be available within five to six days and the results provided to myself and Doctor Mancetti. My office will then contact you concerning a follow-up appointment."

Doctor Stuart told James it would be acceptable for him to leave now, and he also suggested he return home and rest for the balance of the day. He told him to restrict his right arm movements for at least two days to allow the surgical incision to begin the healing process.

"You should be fine to resume your normal activities after a couple of days and if there appears to be any concern or extensive redness or pain in the area, do not hesitate to call my office," said Doctor Stuart.

James thanked the doctor, left the office to begin his journey home.

Doctor Stuart then handed the petri dish containing the remains of the removed growth immediately to his nurse and left the room and returned to his office.

He then telephoned Dr. Mancetti but he was unable to reach him and so he left him a message. "Doctor, you're suspected preliminary diagnosis is confirmed and it is serious but the extent of how serious will not be available for another five to six days. I removed the growth but until we have the laboratory biopsy results, there can be no prognosis. I will personally inform you whenever the results are available. However, my professional experience tells me, it is very serious based upon the thickness and coloration of the growth."

16 CHAPTER

After his transfer from the LA offices to CMP's Irvine offices, Doctor Viking began self-examination of himself to question his actions and behavior towards minorities. He had begun to realize his intentional actions could have fatal results.

He continued to question himself, why did I do it? I am a licensed doctor, and I could have very easily been held responsible for the heart attack patient I failed to diagnose properly. What do I have to gain from this abusive behavior? Why do I not like minorities? They have never abused me, so why?

Neither African Americans, Asians nor Hispanics had ever done anything wrong to him. To his mother maybe, but not to him and yet maybe subconsciously, he resented his mother for ignoring him in favor of one of her low life friends. He had to remind himself, all of this had occurred years ago, not yesterday.

He knew many African Americans, Asians and Hispanics practiced in the medical field and they all acted professionally and performed competently as nurses, doctors and even hospital administrators. His thoughts continued to raise many more questions but still, regarding his abusive behavior, no logical answers magically appeared.

So why do I have this dislike? This phobia? Why the game playing with the patients' lives? I am still a doctor and to many of these same people, I am a person of importance and wasn't becoming important my goal?

Isn't it I who took an oath to treat and heal all without prejudice to anyone? Do I want to lose my career over actions and behavior, which I can control? Don't I like the life the medical field allows me to live? Why, I ask why?

He was sitting alone in his fancy condo close to the beach when he became overcome by all these thoughts. He just sat and stared but saw nothing and for the first time in his life which he could remember, he began to feel remorse. His body ached, he shuddered, and his chest throbbed as remorseful thoughts quickly replaced evil ones. Tears gathered in his eyes, and he truly felt sorry for his actions.

How do I atone? How can I turn bad and evil thoughts into good deeds? I can change, God. I know I can. Help me please. Help me please and I will do good; I promise, I will do good.

Lionel had never in his life been exposed to any religion and now he began invoking the name of God. What could have possibly brought me to do this, he wondered? Am I a miracle in process? Is God suddenly revealing himself to me? Is this what they mean by rebirth? Again, many questions but no answers.

All the questioning and doubt within Lionel took place in a span of about one hour. He became aware of the sun setting and the bright sunlight beaming through his window brought him back to reality. Am I dreaming he wondered, or have I been given the opportunity to change my ways?

The entire event tired him out and he went to lie on the bed and quickly fell into a deep sleep.

The next morning, Lionel arrived at the office uncharacteristically early, he said good morning to everyone he met. Something had transformed him overnight as if a magic wand had anointed him and his entire persona changed.

He became a serious critic of his performance and strove to treat every patient and staff member equally. His tone of voice and conversation with everyone was more positive and the entire staff recognized a changed person.

For the first time since he became a doctor, when he did not fully understand a medical issue, he consulted with other staff doctors on a variety of patient ills until he was satisfied, he had obtained the correct diagnosis for the patient.

The days turned into weeks, and he performed professionally and competently for all patients and medical personnel within the Irvine offices.

However, as time passed, periodically Lionel would again revert to his prior persona. He acted like an old golfer who has been trying to redo his swing and while out on the golf course often finds himself slipping back into his old bad habits.

The result is never good in either golf or medicine and James Spencer can attest to it.

17
CHAPTER

Exactly five days after James had his appointment with Doctor Stuart, he received a call from CMP asking if he could meet with Doctor Mancetti within the next couple of days. James had been dreading this call and advised the caller of his availability any day and at a time most convenient for them. They confirmed the appointment for ten am the very next day.

Not knowing the results of the biopsy, James could only fear the worse and decided he should call his eldest daughter to accompany him, as he did not want to face this situation alone.

He had always tried to be very protective of his children and although he felt this news was his to face alone, reluctantly he dialed his daughter's number. The telephone rang twice before Jill answered it.

"Hi, dad, what's up?"

"Jill, I need a favor from you. I haven't mentioned this to you before or to your sister and brother, but I have been undergoing some medical procedures recently including a biopsy for a possible cancerous growth on my arm. I believe it is serious and I have an appointment tomorrow at ten o'clock at the CMP office here in Irvine to discuss the results of a biopsy taken last week. I would appreciate your accompanying me as quite frankly, I am very nervous and stressful now and will probably be more so tomorrow."

"Dad, why haven't you told us about this before now?" Immediately, Jill realized she had said the wrong thing to her father. "Sorry, dad, you don't have to answer the question. I'll pick you up at 9:45. Would you please come for dinner tonight and we can talk about it?"

"Thanks for the offer, Jill but I am tired as I haven't been getting much sleep lately. I am going to take a sleeping pill soon and I hope I can eliminate some of my doomsday thoughts and get some sleep tonight. We'll have time to talk tomorrow, and I will explain everything to you. Thanks, honey for your understanding and concern."

"Love you, Dad. Try to get a good night's rest. I'll see you tomorrow morning."

As promised, Jill was promptly at her dad's house at 9:45 and found her dad waiting outside for her. He looked older, tired, and depressed. She had never seen her father in this condition.

"Dad, Are you okay?"

"Yes, and no. I took the sleeping pill and slept decently until about four a.m. and then I awoke and just couldn't erase all sorts of fantasies from my head. Jill, I really feel very stressed and nervous. I am not sure why, but I just sense the worst. I am so happy you are here with me."

"Dad, I love you and will help you and so won't Pam and Mason. They were real concerned when I spoke to them last night. You helped all of us through a good portion of our lives and perhaps it is time for us to pay back some old debts."

"Thanks Jill."

Within a few minutes, they had arrived at the medical offices. Jill parked the car and father and daughter slowly walked to the entrance and entered the lobby. James signed the appointment book and took a seat besides Jill. Within five minutes, they were escorted to Doctor Mancetti's office, and he greeted them at the door. James introduced his daughter as they entered.

"James, Jill, please come in and sit down. Jill I am glad to meet you and I am happy you are here to support your father. I realize this is not an easy time for him."

As James and his daughter sat in front of Doctor Mancetti's desk, the Doctor crossed the room and gently closed the door. He quickly returned to his desk but before he was even seated, James began to speak.

"Not good news, is it, Doctor?" Having said this, James fidgeted in his seat awaiting the doctor's reply. Jill took one of his hands and held it tight as she could sense the stress building within her father.

"No, it's not, James, but at this time neither Doctor Stuart nor myself have a sufficient diagnosis to fully determine if it is as bad as you might think or as good as we would hope."

"The growth on your forearm was a type of skin cancer called, Melanoma and the excision, the biopsy, performed by Doctor Stuart to remove it and the subsequent pathology provided the proof of Melanoma. Doctor Stuart is very confident he removed all visible portions of the growth."

Continuing, Doctor Mancetti said," What we do know and what still must be determined is the type of melanoma and the stage it has reached. Knowing the type of cancer will determine if the cancer spread beyond what we can visually confirm and how far within your body has it traveled."

"James, right now, you are a borderline case because the thickness of the sample removed was approximately one millimeter which is the borderline between primary and Mastastic melanoma. Thus, the two questions we need to answer are the type of melanoma and has it spread beyond the removed portion?

The medical community recognizes four types of Melanomas but at this point we can concern ourselves with only two types because of their being found frequently on the arms or upper torso of the elderly.

The description of the two types of melanomas most concerning to us: lentigo maligna and nodular melanoma.

To gain a better and more complete understanding of the information now available to us as doctors, we need you to undergo an additional series of tests which involve additional biopsies but this time, we will be removing portions of selected lymph nodes.

James, in my discussion with Doctor Stuart, He'd like to start the testing soon as possible, and he asked if tomorrow morning would be acceptable to you?"

James shook his head still fearful of the words he had just heard, and he agreed to the further testing. After confirming another appointment with Doctor Stuart, Doctor Mancetti expressed his concern and assured James; he and Doctor Stuart would do everything they could possibly do to work towards a cure for him.

He recommended James begin taking medication targeted at reducing his stress and he gave James a prescription for this medication, and he also advised him to begin using it daily. He then said his goodbyes. James with Jill in tow quickly left Doctor Mancetti's office.

They sat still in the car a long time trying to digest what they had been told by the doctor and thinking of all the possible ramifications to each of their lives. Could the possibility exist for his life to be cut short because of a faulty diagnosis? Why me he wondered? Why did this happen to me?

Jill was almost as shocked as her father. Concerned about losing her father after losing her mother almost two years ago. When a car pulled into the parking space besides their car, they became aware of their surroundings but neither one could say certainly how long they had been sitting there.

Jill suggested they return home, and they could talk there, where it was more comfortable. She drove to her father's home still in a semi-daze, still silent and unsure of what was next.

At the house, they sat in the den and Jill began to ask her father various questions about the growth and for how long he suspected he had a problem.

"Jill, I have been remiss in not telling any of you about this problem. It probably has been more than six months. You see my old doctor convinced me it wasn't a problem, and it became easy for me to accept the explanation. I convinced myself there wasn't a problem. Well, it made two of us wrong and the result is the diagnosis we both heard today spoken by Doctor Mancetti."

"Dad, I am sorry this has happened to you but, Dad you can be assured your children will stand by your side and help you through this problem. I am very sorry, but I must leave now to pick up Susan.

I will stop at the drug store to get your prescription filled and I will return later. You get some rest and I'll be back very soon. I will also call Pam and Mason to see if they can also be here soon."

Jill touched her father's shoulder lightly and left the house. She knew, she now bore the burden of telling her brother and sister plus her extended family.

"I guess as we age, life tosses issues to us for which we are never fully prepared," she said aloud. She then started her car to go and pick up her daughter.

18 CHAPTER

Once Jill had left, James knew he would have a difficult time resting so he decided to call his brother and share his news with him. He knew that Bob was less emotional and could guide him carefully through this ordeal. Bob's wife Marge answered the phone: happy to hear from James.

"James, how are you? How are all the kids and grandkids?" James's answer was a bit somber, "Fine Marge, I must talk to Bob. Is he home?"

"James, you sound like you have lost your best friend. Are you all, right?"

"Sorry Marge, but no I'm not all right, I have learned from my doctor, I have cancer. I am sorry but I am rather emotional now and probably overreacting. Is Bob available?"

"I'm sorry James; I'll find Bob for you right away."

Bob received the news from his wife and suddenly he had visions of his brother dying and he could not help him. He picked up the telephone and began to gather his emotions before he spoke to James.

"James, Marge told me of your problem. Tell me what you know and let me try to help you."

James began to speak, and Bob could sense the uneasiness and stress in his brother's voice. "I've been diagnosed with a form of Melanoma but until I undergo further tests, the doctors cannot provide any additional information as to the prognosis. I am currently dazed over this news and quite frankly, I need some guidance, some direction and I guess a shoulder to lean on."

I'll help any way I can, James. You will not walk through this ordeal alone. If you can, answer a couple of questions for me."

"I will try, Bob but my emotions are under attack at this moment."

"I understand, James but maybe talking will ease a little of the burden you carry. What test did the doctor perform to give you this diagnosis?"

"Remember when we last talked, I told you my primary care doctor was sending me to a dermatology specialist. Well, the dermatologist inspected the growth and then performed surgery to remove it. The purpose was not only to remove the growth but also to perform a biopsy and to analyze the removed material" said, James. "The removed growth was sent to a lab about five days ago and the results were given to Jill and me today by my primary care doctor."

"James, I want you to think a moment about when you first noticed this so-called growth on your arm. Furthermore, how long was it before you pointed out the growth to your doctor?"

"Bob, I really am not sure when I first noticed the spot. Maybe February or March and I think I mentioned it to the doctor about that time. He dismissed it as an age-related spot and when I asked him about it again in May, he again stated it was an age-related thing and gave me a prescription for some cream to treat it. It really wasn't a big concern to me until the itching and soreness began."

"So, James, you have known about this growth for about nine months and if I recall you began to express some concern about it within the last month or so. Is this right? "

James quickly answered, "Yes, that is right. However, I trusted my doctor. Why should I have not believed him?"

"James, you're right, but is the doctor who gave you this recent diagnosis the same doctor who had been seeing you all those months?"

Again, James quickly answered, "No, the original doctor was transferred to another office, and it was my new doctor who made the discovery."

"When are you seeing the doctor again?"

"Which, Doctor?"

"The dermatologist."

"Tomorrow."

"That is good, James. I want you to do a couple of things for yourself. One, listen to your doctors and start getting involved in learning about your condition. Ask many questions and try to understand the purpose of what your doctors are prescribing for you. Two, call me frequently and let me know what tests and treatments are being prescribed and the possible prognosis. I will bounce this off some doctor friends of mine, just to get more opinions. Is this okay with you? "

"Sure."

Before James could say more, Bob said, "James, I strongly suggest you find a legal firm who exclusively practices medical malpractice cases. Tap into some of your executive contacts at Windstep. They should be able to help you. From what you have told me, I believe you have been misdiagnosed by your original doctor."

"Thanks, Bob, I understand and need all the help I can get. I'll give you updates as things progress. I feel much better having spoken to you but I'm tired now and need some rest. Jill and possibly the other children will be here soon and tomorrow I am starting some more tests to determine if the cancer has spread and to learn about possible treatment scenarios."

"James, again I am sorry. Try to get some rest now; I will call you again tomorrow. Perhaps, you'll feel better."

19
CHAPTER

After Jill had left her father's house, she drove to the library to pick up Susan and then to the drug store to arrange to get the prescription ordered by Doctor Mancetti for her father. She only had to wait about ten minutes to receive the prescription but during the wait, she did get the opportunity to talk with her brother Mason and her sister Pam to provide them the sad news of her father's condition. She took on the responsibility of ensuring her family; she would assume responsibility for being with their father for all doctor appointments and tests.

Within hours after receiving the doctor's news, Jill had gotten over the sudden shock of finding out her father had cancer and had shifted her attention to understanding more about the disease.

Jill was very computer literate and began her own research via the Internet. She immediately learned the disease can be manageable with early detection and treatment and most patients have good survival rates dependent on the stage of the cancer.

In James's case, his stage had not yet been determined and the additional testing although starting tomorrow, would not yield answers for many days or even weeks.

Thus, her fear was yet to be determined, for until they knew the results of the additional tests, a prognosis as to the potential survival rate for James was impossible.

She clearly understood Doctor Viking had made a gross mistake and this delayed diagnosis was going to cause her father and the rest of the family much pain and stress. But her major concern at this time was to get her father on the path to where a cure might become possible. Doctor Viking will become the priority later.

The next day, Jill drove her car to her father's house to accompany him to his appointment with Doctor Stuart. James had been waiting for Jill outside of the house. Again, he looked stressed and had lost some of his healthy color. He greeted Jill and entered the car for the relatively short ride to the doctor's office complex. Jill and her father made some small talk while in the waiting room to pass the time, but Jill could plainly see the stress on her father's face.

James had not slept too much last night as his mind wondered from a dire and ominous future to a complete cure and a future life. Hence, when the nurse called his name and escorted him and his daughter into an outpatient surgical room, his tension increased.

There he found Dr. Stuart and introductions were exchanged. A new doctor had joined Doctor Stuart and he quickly introduced him.

"James, this is Doctor Whetland. He is an oncologist and together with Doctor Mancetti, we will be the team working for you."

"Today, we will start by doing some additional biopsies of your lymph nodes and based upon the results, we will then decide upon the appropriate treatment plan. Does this sound okay with you, James?"

"Doctor, the seriousness of my condition is well etched in my brain, and I will try my best to be an informed and trusting patient. After all, based on the diagnosis, I believe if I don't attack the condition soon my life will quickly end. We can start now but please; I would appreciate if you could provide me with details about your actions and what is to be learned and what treatments will possibly help me."

"James, Doctor Whetland, Doctor Mancetti, and I want only to rid you of this disease, and we will gladly share all our thoughts and actions with you. It is good you have the desire and intelligence to learn about it and it will help in your treatment to keep a positive outlook. Doctor Whetland can provide you a summary of what we intend to do today."

"I am glad your daughter is here with you today, James to support you. During the treatment phase, you will require support both emotionally and physically. I want you to understand Doctor Stuart and I have concern for you and will do our best to try to heal you. It is our primary purpose as doctors."

"Today, we will perform a number of biopsies on various lymph nodes all located in your underarm area. This location is the most logical place to determine how far the cancer has moved. By observing the size of the lymph node and then dissecting it, we can provide a more precise diagnosis."

"We will start on what we describe as a sentinel lymph node or very simply, the lymph node closest to the malignant growth previously removed by Doctor Stuart. We will then move further away from the growth to obtain addition sections of other lymph nodes."

Doctor Whetland continued. "By dissecting and analyzing each lymph node, we can determine if the growth has spread to other body parts or vital organs. The results provide the guidelines for treatment but until they are clearly identified, we are not able to make a sound medical diagnosis or prognosis and our objective is to have very sure positive answers for both the diagnosis and prognosis based on sound medical evidence."

"Thanks, Doctor for the explanation," said James. "I am nervous and apprehensive, but ready whenever you are."

"Now, Jill if you do not mind, we must ask you to leave the room and return to the waiting area. This procedure will probably take twenty to thirty minutes and then we want your dad to rest for a short period, as we will be administering a mild sedative to sedate him. We will come to get you after the procedure is complete and you can join your dad while he recuperates from the sedation," said Doctor Stuart. And Jill quietly left the room.

James was now asked to lie on the surgical table to allow Doctor Whetland to administer the sedative. Then, Doctor Whetland assisted by Doctor Stuart, began to obtain biopsies not only on the sentinel lymph node but also on other selected lymph nodes in the general vicinity of the growth. After about twenty minutes, they had completed all the procedures and collected the necessary specimens for the lab analysis.

James continued to lie on the surgical table to recover from the sedation and to rest before being released to go home.

Before leaving the room, Doctor Stuart assured him, Jill would soon be with him, and the mild sedative would wear off in about twenty minutes. The results would be known in four to six days and once available, they would be discussed with James. We will arrange future appointments with Doctors Mancetti and Whetland to discuss and begin the possible treatments.

About forty-five minutes later, James was capable of walking on his own and with the help of Jill returned to their car to make the short quiet drive to James's house.

The ordeal had tired him, and he knew he had to rest but he still had thoughts of a battle he might not win. The four to six days wait to learn of the biopsy results only increased his anxiety and more dire thoughts of his condition. No matter how hard he tried, he could only see himself suffering pain, mental anguish and gradually dying.

20
CHAPTER

James spent the next few days in a mild depressive state. He had difficulty sleeping. Yet at times he remained in bed for many hours as depression took hold of his mind and body. While awake, thoughts of pain and death occupied his time and when he did sleep, his dreams became horrid scenes associated with pain and death. Cancer had taken over his physical and psychological life.

He had discussed his diagnosis with his children in detail and the probabilities of either being cured or dying because of Melanoma.

Their support was unquestionable, and they offered to help in any way possible. Jill promised to do a search of treatments, therapies, new drugs being used and would also try to determine what experimental options were available within the United States. Pam and Mason and the older grandchildren would divide up household chores to assist James and allow him to conserve his energy and fully concentrate on his recovery. All this support from his children and grandchildren boosted James' spirit and gave him a spark of hope.

Meanwhile, James had again spoken to his brother and again Bob suggested he locate an attorney in the Orange County area who specialized in medical malpractice to determine if he had suitable cause for bringing action against Doctor Viking. James promised Bob he would talk to some of his friends at Windstep Electronics and try to obtain a legal recommendation.

As promised, Dr. Stuart's office called on the fifth day and arranged for James to meet with him and Doctor Whetland the next day. First, he told James the cancer had not spread and had remained localized. Still, he said extensive treatment was required to stop the cancer from spreading. He assured James that he had spoken to Doctor Mancetti about their findings and possible treatment plans, and everything would be presented to him tomorrow.

It was another long night for James, but he was happy to learn the cancer had not spread and he would now be on the road to recovery. Jill was again meeting him in the morning and would be driving him to his appointment.

He tried to have positive thoughts while waiting outside his home for Jill to arrive and take him to Doctor Stuart's office. As always, Jill was on time and as she helped him into the car, she noted his apprehension and a sense of sadness.

Within twenty minutes, they drove into the medical building parking lot, parked the car, and walked together to the reception area. They entered the waiting room and Jill could still sense her father's anxiety and stress.

They did not have a long wait before a nurse came out to the waiting room and led him and his daughter into Doctor Stuart's office. Doctor Whetland was also present and both doctors appeared to be very somber. Immediately, this again raised James's apprehension level.

21
CHAPTER

Doctor Stuart was the first to speak. "James, I must be very frank. Although we see the results as somewhat positive, they were not totally encouraging. As I explained to you on the telephone yesterday, the good news is the cancer has not metastasized and has not attached itself to other body organs. Yet it still is localized, and we consider you a borderline case. If we can begin treatments very soon, we have a good opportunity to eliminate the cancer and stop the potential spread to other body parts. We must attack the specific locations of where we now know the cancer is located, if we are to improve your survival possibilities."

"Patients with similar diagnosis have a 65 percent survival rate after five years. With the treatment regimen we are advising, our objective is to make sure you are in the 65 percent category. We understand it is not the best news to give you, but we must be open and honest with you."

Doctor Whetland picked up where Doctor Stuart left off. "James, Jill, it is not the type of news any doctor wants to give his patient. We understand the difficulty for both of you currently and what possibilities exist in the future. However, we still only have a small bit of the information required to adequately determine what therapies might provide the most benefit. We need to do additional tests so we can further localize the areas to attack and how to attack them."

Jill was the first to speak. "Doctor, what if the cancer had metastasized?"

"Jill, under that condition, the five-year survival rate drops to 15 percent. Your father's prognosis is significantly better and yet we realize even this is a difficult prognosis to absorb. I can assure you; we will do everything possible to the extent of our medical knowledge to help your dad."

"Thank you, Doctor."

"The tests we planned for today will take maybe up to two hours but unlike laboratory results, the information we seek will be on film and using the computer, we can relatively quickly assess what damage if any has occurred in the areas under consideration. We could then begin treatments as early as tomorrow and from our perspective, the earlier the better. My initial thoughts involve a combination of therapies involving limited radiation and selective chemotherapy."

After hearing this, James, and Jill both sat stone faced as if both had been struck by lightning. Except, lightning might have been less painful, and death would have come quickly. Now James knew he faced painful days and nights along with his constant thought process and all its deadly endings. Likewise, Jill immediately grasped what the doctors were saying. It was as if her father had been sentenced to death.

"James, can we get you some water or maybe a cup of coffee," asked Doctor Stuart.

"What about you, Jill?"

James staring down at the floor softly answered in a muted tone. "No, I am just in a fog now. All my positive thoughts have been swept away."

Jill also declined the offer from Doctor Stuart.

22
CHAPTER

"James, we are sorry, truly sorry. We discussed beginning additional testing today. But, if you do not feel up to it, we can wait a day or two. Not much longer." Doctor Stuart stayed silent to allow both James and Jill to gather their thoughts and composure.

Jill spoke first. "Dad, maybe we should go home and let this settle in for a day. I am sure all your energy has been sapped by this revelation."

After a minute or so, James assured Jill he did not need additional time to decide and agreed it was probably best to begin testing quickly. He assured both doctors although he was still somewhat dazed, he would gradually be okay, but he did have some questions to ask them.

"Doctor, you mentioned radiation and chemotherapy as possible treatments. Can you explain to me the side effects I might encounter and how it will affect my daily life," asked James.

"James, I believe Doctor Whetland is better qualified to answer that question."

Doctor Whetland thought for a moment or two before speaking.

"James, Jill, I am glad you brought up this question and it should be of concern to both of you. Cancer treatments of any type are never easy. They affect your entire body both mentally and physically and dependent on how extensive the disease has progressed will determine the length of time you will be affected."

"As I mentioned earlier, the treatment of choice will be a combination of low dosage radiation applied to the affected area and maybe two or three types of chemotherapy applications. Depending on patient response, these treatments may be administered over a period of two to six months followed by a continuous follow-up program which may include additional biopsies and MRI scans."

"This will be the treatment regimen, and now for the potential side effects. It seems each person undergoing these procedures has similar responses to the treatments but whereas one patient always feels tired, the other patient suffers from nausea and the third patient has skin issues. Hence, all I can tell you is you can expect to have one overriding issue or quite a few."

"I can assure you at times it will be tough to bear. We

will provide medications to try and minimize the side effects for you. In time, the side effects will gradually pass as you move towards having a healthier body.

"There are a number of precautions you should take to minimize the side effects. Doctor Stuart, will now provide some caveats to adhere to during the treatment period."

"Thanks Doctor. James, during the treatment period, there are certain guidelines we want you to follow and Jill to assist your father, you also must have an awareness of these guidelines."

1. Be sure to get plenty of rest and sleep. Fatigue will become your worst enemy during the treatment period and for several weeks beyond the end of the treatments. If, you need medication to sleep, we will provide you prescriptive drugs.
2. It is highly recommended you eat a well-balanced diet. This will help you fight some of the fatigue and provide your system with much needed nourishment. We will provide you with a diet recommendation.
3. The skin in the area where radiation will be applied will become very sensitive, look sunburned and more than likely be painful. Do not use any products on this skin area unless it is listed in the skin care booklet, we will provide to you.

4. Because your skin will be sensitive, do not wear any tight-fitting shirts or other garments while undergoing the radiation treatment.
5. Do not cover the sensitive skin area with any type of bandage or gauze unless it is also listed in the skin care booklet.
6. Avoid rubbing or scratching this area.
7. Do not apply heat or cold to the area. Use only lukewarm water to wash the area.
8. Lastly avoid exposing the affected skin area to the sun.
9. Talk to your friends and family about your feelings to reduce the chance of prolonged depression.
10. Keep Doctor Whetland and I informed about any changes you experience, or you sense in your bodily functions.

"We will have many more meetings with you along with providing you numerous booklets regarding your treatments. However, I have just been informed the Radiology Laboratory is waiting for you so we can continue this conversation later and more than likely, we will see you in the next day or two to begin the treatments."

Within a couple of minutes, the nurse reentered the room to take James to the radiology labs where various scans would be taken to visually dissect the questionable lymph nodes. The doctors needed complete detailed images on twenty to thirty lymph nodes situated in and around the growth area and complete photographic details were required, one frame at a time.

The process for James was more than two hours long, tiring and very uncomfortable. James persevered and during the time he was within the MRI and CAT SCAN chambers, he tried to focus his thoughts not on his cure but rather on retribution. Hate for Doctor Viking began to build for creating the condition he now faced and for all his pain and the pain Doctor Viking had thrust upon his family. He wanted retribution for what he now felt was a possible death sentence.

When the testing was over, he called his daughter to meet him at the radiology lab and when she arrived, she found him tired and agitated. With the aid of a nurse and a wheelchair, they helped him to the car. With Jill driving and James's resting, together they left for the short but very sad drive home.

23
CHAPTER

When they arrived at the house, her father appeared to have regained his composure and for whatever reason, his daughter felt he had a look of determination. Maybe she thought or subconsciously hoped, he will beat the odds.

James told Jill it was okay to leave him alone as he was tired and needed to get some rest. She agreed and left within a few minutes after checking a few things in the kitchen to ensure her dad at least had some food for his dinner. “Dad, I will call you later and if you need me sooner, just call. I am leaving now, please try to get some rest.”

In wasn’t more than three minutes after Jill had left the house that James was speaking on the telephone to the President of Windstep Electronics. “Fred, how are you?”

“I am fine James. How are you doing?”

“I have a serious medical issue and because of how it has been handled, I am confident I need some legal help.” James briefly explained his medical situation to Fred and then asked him, “I would appreciate if you would talk to the corporate attorney and get me the name or names of some competent medical malpractice attorneys in the area?”

“I’ll absolutely do it; James and I am sorry to hear you are not doing well. I should be able to get back to you either later today or the first thing in the morning.”

“Thanks, Fred. Your help is really appreciated.”

"James, you served us well for a long time and you are not asking me to do very much. However, if you need additional information or help, please call me at any time either in the office or at my home. We have a strong group of people here who all know you and would be perfectly happy to help you."

"Thanks, Fred."

"Bye, James. I'll have information for you very soon."

James slowly laid the telephone down and sighed. He had started down the path of retribution, and he knew it may be a long and bumpy road, but he wasn't going to allow either his illness or stress to get in his way.

24
CHAPTER

As promised the president of Windstep Electronics returned James' call within a few hours after James had called him. He gave James one name and assured James this person was the best medical malpractice litigator in Orange County. He had questioned both his in-house counsel and a close attorney friend. Both attorneys had only one name, Hope Moran.

James thanked Fred and tried to settle in for another long and stressful night. He could feel the cancer slowly sapping life out of him and his hatred for Doctor Viking grew. He tried watching television, but his thoughts kept bringing up scenarios of bedridden images of a dying man.

As he had anticipated, James had another restless night filled with nightmares and when he awoke early, he tried to maintain his normal activities, but it was not possible. About 9:30 a.m., he called the office of Hope Moran and after a brief ten-minute discussion with her about the sequence of events, which lead up to, his existing condition, she agreed to meet him to discuss the probable issue and they arranged an appointment for later in the week.

Although he was still depressed and weak, he was glad he was able to get a quick appointment with this attorney. Out loud he said, "Doctor Viking, I am out to get you and I will find a way to retribution. You won't be able to hide anywhere."

25
CHAPTER

Three days later, James entered the offices of Hope Moran for step one of his retribution agenda.

The professionally decorated reception area of the legal practice had an aura of success. James knew from his prior discussion with the President of Windstep Electronics, the practice of Hope Moran's firm was solely dedicated to medical malpractice litigation. Hope Moran had the reputation of being aggressive, skillful, and highly regarded within the Orange County legal community.

The appointment was scheduled for ten o'clock and the receptionist led him into Hope's office almost exactly at the appointed time.

Her inner office decorated in a similar theme to the reception area; conservative with richly paneled walls; part of which was covered with rows of legal books neatly aligned on long bookshelves. Fresh flowers adorned the desk and James noticed pictures of a couple and three smiling children in frames on the credenza behind her desk. When he entered the office, Hope rose from her desk and introduced herself. "I think we will be more comfortable over here" she said inviting him to move to the couch, while she sat in a nearby armchair. When they were comfortably seated, she began to speak.

"Mr. Spencer or if I might, call you James, based upon our prior telephone conversation, I have several questions to ask you, but first, I want you to understand today's meeting is at no cost to you. There is no obligation on your behalf, financial or otherwise and it will be your decision to continue or to engage me to represent you, if we both decide it is in your best interest to continue with litigation.

Depending on how you answer my questions, will initially allow me to determine if we have a case. I know you told me you had been diagnosed with Melanoma and it was at a Stage III or localized level. I also understand you are receiving both radiation, chemotherapy and other drug therapies and will continue to do so for another six months or longer. Is this correct?"

James had been listening intently and quickly answered, "Yes, it is Stage III, and it is localized to the lymph nodes closest to where the growth was on my right forearm.

Doctor Whetland, my assigned oncologist, has me on a twice a week routine including radiation once weekly and chemotherapy twice weekly. As part of the chemo treatment, I also am taking Interferon. Tomorrow is my double dosage day as I call it, for both radiation and Interferon."

"Well, James, let's hope your treatment will be successful but I would be remiss if I didn't inform you, medical malpractice is always the most difficult type of case to try in California and in many other states. It is a difficult challenge to bring before the court. The difficulty extends also to every attorney wanting to go forward with a case, because there must be clear and convincing evidence of neglect or negligence before any attorney will agree to continue with litigation."

Continuing, Hope Moran provided a short definition of medical malpractice for James. "Medical malpractice is defined as professional negligence by act or omission by a health care provider in which the treatment provided to the patient falls below the normal accepted standard of practice within the medical community and which results in either injury or death to the patient."

"In essence James, this is what we must prove. The care provided to you did not meet the standard offered to other patients with similar conditions."

"There is also another issue you must be aware of as a California resident. California law limits the amount of

awards for non-economic issues to $250,000 and caps the attorney fees accordingly. There is no limit on punitive damages. Hence, James, we may have a great case but with the possibility of no compensation after legal fees unless you are awarded punitive damages."

"So, not only do we have the challenge of proving negligence, the costs of evidence discovery, the costs for expert witnesses and court costs may approach the maximum award if we win the case."

"However now, I'd like to hear your story and the financial factors we can deal with later. So how about giving me your story beyond what we briefly discussed on the telephone. I need to know the chronological history of events, your feelings, your motivation and what do you expect to gain if your claim meets what I call; the smell test."

26
CHAPTER

Hope could see that James was a little agitated and yet, this is exactly what she wanted. People often let their emotions loose when they are agitated. It was a trick she acquired in law school from a professor who taught cross-examination.

"To start, I am bitter and angry. I trusted my doctor only to learn too late he had misled me and now I am forced to pay the price. A very large price for my family and me. I was led down a rose-colored path by Doctor Viking convincing me about age spots which somehow magically developed into Stage III Melanoma."

Continuing, James became a little more emotional. "Now you want to know what do I want? I am not interested in money and this economic cap does not bother or worry me. What I really want is retribution. I want this Lionel Viking, who so calls himself a doctor, banned from practicing in this state or anywhere else ever again. No person or family should have to suffer at any time the way I am now suffering both physically and mentally. Lastly, I know this is only the beginning of my suffering, the worse for me is yet to come and even after all the treatments, the outcome remains cloudy."

"Wow" said Hope. "That is a big ax you're carrying, and I can understand your wanting the doctor's head. Yet, from the minimal amount of information you gave me over the phone, you were somewhat remiss in believing what your doctor told you and not questioning him to give you a more plausible explanation; something you could understand. You repeatedly accepted without a peep, sunspots, and age spots."

"You told me on the telephone it was sore at times and maybe growing? You clearly recognized the damn thing wasn't going away, yet for whatever reason, you avoided asking the important questions to get the answers which made sense to you or even getting a second opinion from another doctor."

"If I take this case, the people we will go against are ruthless. They honestly don't care if you are going to live or die."

"They have a big important client to protect, a corporation who doesn't want the publicity, an insurance company who doesn't want to pay and a sizable bonus waiting for them for winning the case."

"They will work every angle from every direction, every minute to twist your story and try to prove to the judge and jury you are to blame for allowing time to elapse without pushing for a plausible explanation of your condition. In other words, they will push very hard to prove, you can only blame yourself, not your HMO."

James quickly said. "Look Mrs. Moran, maybe I was a little lax in my approach but isn't there a sense of trust we have towards all our professionals? I was an engineer and people expected me to know electronics and when I signed my name to a design, people expected it to function per the design. In other words, they trusted me as a professional."

"Hence, the reason I am here is because a professional deceived me. I want to have my say in court and quite frankly, I'm upset that a system I put my faith in and whose stated objective is to heal me, has failed me. The system has failed me badly. I don't want it to fail others and it is why I am here meeting with you today."

"Okay, James, you have convinced me of your seriousness, but, right now, in my opinion, you have a borderline case and before my making a commitment to you, there are many questions requiring answers which to me means, I have work to do. This will take me at least two to three days and then, I will inform you of my decision."

"I cannot think of anything more to say for now. Thank you for considering my firm and I do sincerely wish.

you well in your treatments."

James rose from his chair, shook Hope's hand, and said, "Thank you for your time and for listening to me. I look forward to your call."

When James had closed the door to Hope's office, she sat for a few minutes thinking about Mr. Spencer and the ordeal he was now having to face. She felt there was the possibility of a case, but more evidence was needed before her, or any firm would make a commitment to litigate. More details about the doctor were required and she had the right investigator to obtain those details. She then picked up the telephone to call her lead investigator, Marvin Kushner.

"Marvin, what is your schedule for the next few days?"

"I am not super busy, and I can always give you some time," said Marvin. "Tell me what you need and by when?"

Hope was thankful that Marvin could give her some time. Intuitively, she felt there may be a workable case but if I were to handle this case, based upon Mr. Spencer's current condition, it must be put on a fast track.

"Marvin, I need a complete history on a Doctor Lionel Viking who practices for CMP, probably in Irvine. I have a borderline case, which would involve him, but I need some reasons beyond what my potential client claims before I can decide to continue. Two to three days would work fine for me."

"Your wish is my command, Hope. I still may have a couple of doors I can open at CMP. Let me see if I can get a peek at what maybe behind those doors. I should have some answers in two days, and I will keep you advised."

"Thanks, Marvin."

"Not a problem," said Marvin.

Marvin hung up the telephone and was excited to be working on a medical issue involving a doctor. Medicine was his specialty and although his practicing days went away a long time ago. He knew doctors make mistakes but usually they are minor and have no lasting effect upon the patient. Yet, there is always the chance gross negligence by a physician can result in horrible outcomes for the patient.

His objective now was to separate the fact from fiction and learn something about the Doctor Lionel Viking.

27
CHAPTER

Marvin Kushner had worked for Hope Moran's firm for about two years as an investigator and medical consultant and he was an excellent fit for a medical malpractice attorney. At the time Hope had hired him, she did not realize the extent of the contributions Marvin would bring to her practice. He was an excellent investigator who was very creative on how he obtained information and his medical knowledge was also outstanding. From the time he was hired, it became a win-win situation for both Hope and Marvin.

Marvin had been a classmate and friend of Hope's husband during their college days, and they had remained in close contact with each other over the years. Marvin had gone on to graduate school, then medical school and eventually became a successful physician. Yet as bright as he was, his success lasted only a few years, when his license to practice was formally suspended, after he became addicted to drugs.

It was a long and bumpy road for Marvin and most of it was downhill. His use of drugs destroyed his marriage, his successful practice and himself and eventually he ended up, as just another sorry human being, on skid row. It was there, Hope and her husband found him and rescued him from his habit and finally was able to persuade him to enter a Salvation Army program for alcohol and drug abusers.

Miraculously within months, Marvin became a new person and began to speak of starting a new life, a rebirth. He knew drugs were his demons and would continue to chase and haunt him for a long time, but he felt with the support of friends and the Salvation Army follow-up programs, he could stay on the correct path and create a more satisfying and rewarding life for himself.

He stayed true to his convictions and after about one year and nearing the end of his rehab period; Hope's husband suggested to her, Marvin would be an excellent choice as an investigator and medical consultant for her legal practice. He was a trained physician, he was very bright, and he needed a path which would not only enable him to financially support himself but would keep him occupied, raise his self-esteem, and allow him to reenter mainstream society.

Hope understood Marvin's needs and she knew he was sincere about turning his life around. She felt he would be a perfect fit for her practice as he had the intellect, required to succeed. She knew very few small legal firms who could afford the services of a full-time medical consultant. With this knowledge, she did not hesitate to ask Marvin if he would consider joining her firm. Advising him her practice was growing and she had established a strong legal reputation in Orange County. She assured him she definitely needed someone with medical knowledge who could guide her on the many medical details required to support her cases. She also knew he would serve as a good investigator; something which is always required by most legal practices.

Without any hesitation, Marvin said yes. After all he had been through in the past, Hope and her husband literally had saved his life, and both had remained his good friends even through his worst days. He also realized, it would allow him to practice what he loved most and had been trained to do, medicine, but without having to deal with patients or paperwork, while still stimulating and testing his intellect.

Now two years later, he continued to attend weekly programs operated by the Salvation Army for addicts. He was also able to successfully help the firm with many cases, both in the role of medical consultant and as an investigator. Now he had received the request from Hope to determine, who was Lionel Viking, MD?

Hope had provided Marvin with just a hint of details concerning the doctor and practically nothing about the patient or his condition. Her interest in this doctor was to learn about his background, experience, and his reputation within the medical community. She did not provide any details of the patient beyond he had an illness, which possibly could have been avoided if Doctor Viking had performed to the medical standards of all practitioners.

It troubled Marvin when a doctor had to be confronted on a previous misdeed, which possibly affected a patient's life. He did not know the doctor by name, but he did know Hope was a very detail-oriented attorney who demanded knowing her potential adversaries, in some cases, better than they knew themselves.

It took Marvin less than an hour to plan the investigative steps he would take to obtain the information Hope had requested. He did this without the knowledge of what he was about to learn during his investigation over the next few days and he had no inclination how the investigation would turn out.

28 CHAPTER

Marvin was a bright, resourceful, go-getter type of guy and began his immediate search by way of the Internet. With just a few clicks of the mouse on a few selected web sites, he began to establish a general picture of Doctor Lionel Viking.

He learned Doctor Viking had graduated with a medical degree in 1989 from UCLA, a highly regarded California university and he had performed his residency without incidence at the Los Angeles County Hospital. He had not gone on to specialize in any field and obviously preferred to be a general practitioner and he continued in this specialty after joining CMP in 1991.

The CMP web site had a picture of him along with a brief outline of his credentials. It also showed he was practicing at CMP's Fountain Valley offices.

An online search of the California Medical Board site revealed two incidents of settlements in the last 14 months involving Doctor Viking. He knew medical boards do not publish the whys or when's of these incidents and as such they could be simple or complex medical issues. Additionally, searches of legal sites relating to medical practices showed the doctor had never been named in a medical malpractice suit. On the surface, although there were a couple of blemishes, to Marvin, Doctor Viking appeared to be an average general practitioner.

Marvin knew this information would not be of much practical use to Hope Moran trying to establish a case. Hence, his next option would be to do some networking with his prior contacts within CMP.

During his tenure as a physician, Marvin had known several doctors employed by CMP and periodically he had remained in contact with some of them and he was also socially friendly with one of the department heads. He was hoping someone within the corporation could offer additional information about Doctor Viking beyond the limited amount he already had gathered from his Internet searches.

Early the next morning he called his physician contact at CMP and asked him for some help in obtaining some general information about Doctor Viking. The contact was willing to help him as reciprocation to Marvin.

"What do you need, Marvin?"

"Well, I just want some general information about his work history with CMP. On paper, he appears to be an okay doctor and I just want to know if CMP sees it the same way."

"Give me a few minutes Marvin and let me find out what I can give you. I'll call you back in about ten minutes."

After hanging up, Marvin began to look at data involving Lionel Viking outside of the medical field. He learned Lionel was a very active student during his university days including leading a sit-in against equal opportunity. Marvin brushed the action off as being youthful idealism as no other instances involving Lionel's behavior, either good or bad were publicized.

Within a few minutes, the physician contact at CMP returned his call.

"Marvin, what I am about to tell you is not for publication, but it may help you. Doctor Viking has been transferred between various offices three times in the last three years. It appears, he has had patient complaints about not properly treating Asians, African Americans, and Hispanics. I do not have access to the details, but you know, where there is smoke, you usually find fire. Wish I could help you more."

"Very interesting. Thanks for the information and help. It is a good start and I understand and appreciate what you have done and now, I will try some other avenues."

With the limited information he had thus far obtained and this last piece of controversial information, he decided to call Hope and share this with her to get some response.

"Hope, Marvin here. I am making some progress concerning Doctor Viking." He then went on to provide her a brief outline of the information gathered to-date but specifically leaving out the information he had learned from CMP.

"However, I do have a question for you. What is the ethnicity of your potential client?"

"He is African American, Marvin. Why do you ask?"

"Well, it seems our doctor Viking has had relationship issues with some ethnic patients. I don't know all the details, but I will try to get more answers. Your client maybe another one of his mistreated patients. I'll get back to you in a day or so. Maybe we have identified a doctor with either no bedside manners or very selective ones!"

"Thanks, Marvin. It is beginning to sound interesting and intriguing. Thanks for the information and I look forward to hearing more of the story. Until then, goodbye."

After disconnecting the telephone call to Hope, it didn't take Marvin long to again telephone CMP and ask for another of his contacts.

"John, it's me Marvin. How are you and how is the family?"

"Marvin, you rascal. The family is fine. Glad to hear from you and glad to hear you are staying clean and sober. I met Hope Moran and her husband at a function the other day and they were so happy with your progress. Hope told me you are an important member of her staff. I am damn happy for you. So now, how can I help you?"

"John, there is physician named Lionel Viking on the CMP staff and I understand he has been associated with various offices and I would like to know why all the transfers. Is he being shuffled from office to office for a specific reason or are there some personal issues associated with his frequent interoffice transfers?"

"Hmm, Marvin, those are tough questions which I may have some difficulty answering. I know based upon your association with Hope, it must involve a legal issue."

"You are correct, John, it does, but CMP maybe facing a bigger problem in the future than what possibly exists today. I know CMP's reputation and I am sure the board does not want it to be tarnished because of the actions of one wayward doctor who just happens to be on their staff."

"I understand, Marvin and I also hear what you are not saying; but there are some confidentiality rules in play. I will tell you this, but you will have to fill in the blanks from here on out. There have been two settlements, both settled quickly for not a large amount and sealed to avoid bad press. One involved an Asian and the other a Hispanic patient, both of whom felt Doctor Viking had medically mistreated them. Marvin, you did not hear this from me."

"John thanks for the information and trust me, your name and anyone else at CMP will never be mentioned to my employer or anyone else. I have learned there are legal remedies to get the entire picture. Thank you for your support and help."

"I owe you something but only payable in the future. Please extend my regards to your wife and let's get together for lunch someday soon. My treat."

"I really enjoyed speaking with you, Marvin. Give me a call when you're available for my free lunch."

Marvin laughed as he hung up the telephone call to his CMP contact and spent a few moments digesting the information. He then decided it was time to again call Hope.

"I believe we need a meeting to discuss some interesting revelations involving Doctor Viking."

Hope said, "Hmm, I love mysteries. How is tomorrow around ten?"

"Sounds good to me." Now Marvin began to wonder about this doctor he was now investigating.

29
CHAPTER

About the time Hope was expecting to meet with Marvin, she decided to place a quick call to James. He had been waiting to hear from her firm about the possibility of pursuing litigation against Doctor Viking, as it had been almost one week since he had met Hope at her office.

It was late in the morning. and she found him at home resting after another dual treatment when Hope telephoned him.

"James, I am calling to provide you an update about our recent meeting. It is beginning to appear we may have the possibility of a case, but I am still awaiting additional information on a few issues. I believe, answers to most of my concerns should be forthcoming in the next few days. I will call you by Friday of this week to provide you the latest status and decide on the case. Lastly, I do hope you are doing well with your treatments."

"Thanks, Hope for the call. I do appreciate your concern. I have my good days and my bad ones, but I still do have those strong feelings about Doctor Viking, so I am hoping you take the case. I will be here Friday to receive your call. Again, thanks for the call and your wishes."

The call from Hope lifted James' spirits and he began to sense he was getting closer to finding out why he had been mistreated which would allow him to move on to step two of his retribution agenda.

Meanwhile, Marvin had arrived at Hope's suite of offices, about ten minutes before their scheduled meeting. Since he had last spoken to her, he had assembled all the information he was able to gather about

Lionel Viking. With Hope's legal background combined with his medical knowledge, he was sure they would have enough to analyze the information and draw a consensus of opinions about Doctor Viking.

Hope appeared a couple of minutes later and ushered Marvin into her office. The usual pleasantries were exchanged and after they were both seated; Hope asked Marvin to provide a detailed summary of the information he had gathered about Doctor Viking.

"Here is what I have now. He was an average student at UCLA. Graduated in 1989 with very acceptable grades and was immediately accepted to begin a two-year residency with the LA County Hospital. No news good or bad up to this point."

Marvin, when did he join CMP?" asked Hope.

"He was hired as a general practitioner in 1991 shortly after finishing his residency and started practicing at the West, LA office operated by CMP. Seven months later he was transferred to a larger set of offices in Irvine also as a general practitioner. I am guessing, this was probably where he met your potential client. Yet, after about eight months in Irvine, he was again transferred to another office in Fountain Valley. He is still there today."

"That's good, Marvin but why the transfers and besides, you said there was some other interesting details. Let's hear them now."

"I always save the juicy details for last, Hope." Marvin was laughing as he said it. "Here is what I know. The Medical Board of California lists two settlements involving Doctor Vikings. These incidents are only published when settlements exceed $3000 as required by California codes for medical practices but you never know the size of the settlement nor the reasons for the settlements. This information came from a confidential source who confirmed CMP had been involved in two settlements involving Doctor Viking. More likely, they are the ones published by the medical board as the law clearly states all medical organizations must report such incidences to the board. One incident involved an Asian and the other a Hispanic. I do not know the details of either case as both were settled quickly for a moderate sum and sealed with signed confidential agreements. Considering the knowledge of my source, I would assume the settlements were for malpractice and resulted in the eventual transfers of Doctor Viking between CMP offices."

Marvin continued, "In addition, there is another item I discovered about Doctor Viking during his college days. He led a rally against equal opportunity. I am not sure whether it means youthful idealism or perhaps he has had an issue with minorities for a long time."

Hope sat back and thought for a minute or two and Marvin knew from prior experience she was trying to fit the pieces together to form a rational story from what she had just learned from him.

"Marvin let's you and I play with this for a while. I am beginning to form a picture of Doctor Viking and it is not a pretty one. You said two settlements, one Asian, one Hispanic. Now we have an African American man. Sounds racially charged to me. Discrimination? Mistreatment of minorities! What do you think?"

"What is the diagnosis of the patient?"

"Stage III Melanoma," said Hope.

"Oh no, it is somewhat fortunate but still scary. It means the disease has only progressed locally, to nearby nodes and has not yet metastasized. If it had spread and was diagnosed as Stage IV, then the five-year survival rate would have been 15 percent or less. However, the five-year survival rate for Stage III patients is still only 65 percent, which is still considered medium to high risk."

"Your client has possibly been given a deferred death sentence by the not so good doctor," said Marvin in an almost hushed tone.

Marvin continued, "Hope, African American, Asian, Hispanic. He is a doctor. Color or race should never enter the equation. It does not make any sense to me unless!"

"Unless what Marvin?"

"Unless he hides his true feelings about minorities from everyone except the patient. Even then, he hides it by giving them false or misleading diagnosis and they might not know or discover the difference until it is too late. He gives them a semi-convincing diagnosis, brushes off their concerns and fades away before a true diagnosis is determined."

"Think about your client; Stage III Melanoma, which could be deadly. If he survives this episode, who is to guarantee it will not return within five years and occur again as Melanoma or in another form of more deadly cancer, which in many cases attacks the bones or vital organs. Eventually, Doctor Viking who has taken a solemn oath to serve and save people may end up as a killer."

"Marvin, you have provided me a reasonable assumption and I am convinced we have a reasonable case currently but thus far; it is solely based only upon circumstantial evidence. If you can find a way to shift some of your findings and assumptions from circumstantial to factual evidence, then we have a case; I mean a strong case."

"When or I should say if, the decision is made to go forward, I would like you to meet our client to discuss the medical aspects with him. Until then, I want you to spend the next few days getting to know more about Doctor Viking. Where did he grow up? Did he go to a school full of minorities? Why the hatred? What about his parents, girlfriends, perhaps a wife, kids, classmates, etcetera. We don't have a strong case until circumstantial becomes factual and we have a preponderance of evidence to convince a judge and jury."

Hope emphasized again, "We are almost there but to go forward with a case, I need more, lots more!"

Marvin got the message and understood what was needed. His initial impression of Doctor Viking was not good, and it had just gotten worse. He knew without being told there was much more information he needed to gather and analyze before the firm really got to know Doctor Viking.

Marvin rose and was about to leave the office. His mind had clicked into overdrive as if he was mapping out his approach like a surgeon about to perform open-heart surgery for a Mitral Valve repair.

"Got it, Hope, I'll talk to you as the information becomes available to me. I am sure there are more surprises ahead and a lot more to the story beyond the first chapter."

Hope was a quick reader and was well beyond chapter one. She was already well into the chapters titled negligence and discrimination. One chapter for the civil courts and another for the federal courts.

30 CHAPTER

Marvin left Hope's office and his mind filled with questions. Where do I to start? Who knows what? When was his behavior first recognized? The number of questions unanswered seemed overwhelming but this was his job, and he relished the challenge. It was the job he had chosen to do.

His thoughts shifted to the plight of client and his family. They didn't have a choice and he and his family are now paying the price of pain and suffering. If anything, Marvin said to himself. "Make it right for him." With that last thought in mind, he drove back to his apartment, assured now, he also had an agenda, and he was very good at completing agendas.

He entered his apartment, flipped on lights, and headed for the fridge. He never liked to work on an empty stomach, and he knew today and the days ahead, would be long and stressful. After finishing a peanut butter sandwich, a glass of milk and a couple of raisin oatmeal cookies, he sat at his computer thinking about where he should start. He remembered CMP had a brief introductory of Doctor Viking on their web site. Maybe CMP and the doctor's bio is the place to start.

He typed in the URL for CMP and immediately the home page appeared on his screen. He quickly scanned the usual pictures of facilities and the well-phrased vision of Coastal Medical Practitioners in large print. On the left column was a list of office locations and physicians. He clicked on the physician heading and then scanned down the alphabetical list until he found Doctor Viking. He double clicked on his name and was instantly taken to the introductory presentation of Doctor Viking.

There was a photograph of the doctor with his long hair and his white lab coat along with a short bio. James highlighted the write-up and then clicked on the print option. He wanted a hard copy so he could carefully study what was being written about Doctor Viking.

Doctor Lionel Viking, MD
General Practitioner

Lionel Viking, MD, joined CMP in 1991 as a General Practitioner. A member of CMP's Division of Primary Care Physicians, he received his MD from the University of California in 1989 and completed his residency at Los Angeles County General Hospital in 1991. Currently, he is a Primary Care Physician at CMP's Fountain Valley Facilities. When Doctor Viking is not seeing patients, he enjoys spending time hiking in the many Southern California mountain areas. As a former resident of The City of Compton and alumni of Compton High School, he now makes his home in Orange County.

Short and not so interesting but immediately, bells began to ring in Marvin's head. Compton, an area with a population predominately composed of African Americans, Asians, and Hispanics. LA County General, predominately a hospital for the poor, along with African Americans and Hispanic residents of the surrounding areas.

Hiking, a solitary sport typically enjoyed by loners trying to avoid people and the day-to-day humdrum. Oh my, oh my, what do we have here, thought Marvin?

Now that he knew where Doctor Viking spent his youth, his research just got easier, but he knew from experience, it is always difficult to spot a needle in a haystack until it pricks your finger.

He started by searching the name Viking in LA County. Close to forty names appeared but none of them lived in Compton. He realized he had better use the people search engine used by Hope's firm. It provided excellent details including current and previous residencies. He also realized he needed to narrow the scope of his search. He signed into the site used by most attorneys and typed in.

"Viking, 65 years old, Los Angeles County, California." Now he was seeking the parents of Doctor Viking because he felt this could provide some additional clues about whom he now called, the not so good Doctor.

Suddenly the list he was seeking was reduced to eight people with ages from 55 to 71 years old. He scanned each one carefully as to where they lived now and in the past. He reduced the list to three names who had lived in the Compton area during the time he estimated Doctor Viking was enrolled in High School.

Since Doctor Viking had graduated medical school in 1989, he probably graduated high school in 1980 or 1981. He made a note of this and would use this information to review high school yearbooks in the Compton library within the next day or two.

Next, using another search engine used only by attorneys and public safety personnel, he started a search of legal issues in the Compton area by anyone with the last name of Viking during a period of 1975 until 1985. This involved a search of arrests or police calls in the Compton area during the period in question. The resulting list was not very long but at least two police reports immediately drew Marvin's attention.

The first was written in June of 1977 and involved a domestic disturbance in The City of Compton between Jason, a.k.a. Jazzie Boone and his girlfriend Mary Beth Viking. The girl friend had claimed Jason Boone beat her but later she recanted the charges. No further details were available.

The second offense also involved Jason Boone who had been arrested in 1979 for public drunkenness in the company of a Mary Beth Viking. He spent the night in the Compton jail, but she was set free and again no further details were available.

Marvin made a note of these incidents and his intuition had him believing he had found what he was seeking about Doctor Viking. It would now take some old-fashioned face-to-face investigation time in The City of Compton to learn more about Doctor Viking's past. This could start in the morning but for now he had already worked more than 14 hours and he needed some sleep.

Seven minutes later he was snuggled in his bed, but only bad thoughts were running through in his head.

31

CHAPTER

Marvin slept about ten hours and awakened when the sun ~~light~~ lit up his bedroom. He was still sleepy but rose from the bed and headed for the shower. Knowing he had another busy day ahead for himself, he reminded himself to stick to his agenda. He had no intention of letting Hope or her client down. As an investigator, he knew only thoroughness and accuracy in his search of information and evidence concerning Doctor Viking would result in bringing the case to trial. Hope was very serious when she said, "Beyond a reasonable doubt."

After completing all his necessary personal cleansing chores, he quickly dressed and left his apartment and headed for the parking garage. He drove his car out of the garage to begin his trip to The City of Compton. But within a few minutes of driving, he realized he was hungry, so he pulled his car into the parking lot of a local restaurant to get himself a decent breakfast. A meal and a couple of cups coffee, were always a good start for Marvin.

After breakfast, he went over the two stops he had planned for his day. Compton Library and the local newspaper. ~~yet;~~ Marvin felt if some interesting information.

presented itself, more stops would be added.

He resumed his drive to The City of Compton which would take him about forty minutes to an hour dependent on traffic but during the drive, he would have the time to rethink his schedule and the agenda he had completed last night. The freeway traffic was not so busy on this day and Marvin arrived in The City of Compton in just over forty-five minutes.

First on his agenda was a visit to the local library where he would try to learn about Lionel Viking's high school history. He was able to locate the library by using the Thomas Guide Maps and he was following the route of the yellow highlighted lines he made on the Compton City map the previous night. Within ten minutes after exiting the freeway, he arrived at the Compton main library, drove into the parking lot, parked his car, walked across the parking lot, and entered the library through the large entry doors.

32
CHAPTER

Once inside the library, he looked around for the information desk so he could learn where the library stored high school yearbooks. The desk was close to the entrance, and as he approached the clerk asked for information. "Pardon me ma'am, could you please help me? I am looking for Compton High School yearbooks for the late 1970s' until early 1980s'."

The woman was quick to reply. "I just wish all the questions I get were so easy. Aisle 14, on the right-hand side about halfway downs the aisle on the lower shelves. We probably have more than 30 years of high school yearbooks and they are separated alphabetically by the name of the school. If you need more help, don't hesitate to ask, because it is why I am here every day."

Marvin smiled, thanked the woman, and headed in the direction of aisle 14 and when he got there, he turned the corner and slowly studied the books on the right-hand side. Less than a minute later, he spotted the Compton High School yearbooks on the lower shelf, just as the woman behind the information desk had advised him.

He selected the yearbook copies of 1977, 1978, 1979 and 1980 and carefully removed them from the shelf. He headed towards a nearby vacant table where he could study each book in detail. Yet, he really wasn't sure of what he expected to find but he knew once he found something about Lionel Viking, other pieces of the puzzle may begin to fall into place and lead him along a new path.

There was nothing of interest in either the 1977 or the 1978 book but the old pictures, clothing styles and the young faces amused him. It reminded him of his high school days so long ago. Finishing with the 1978 book, he opened the 1979 book and was startled by what he saw in front of him. A picture of the Class President, Lionel Viking! There, on the first page. A picture of Lionel Viking at 17 years old and in the front of the book. He had been Class President! Wow!

Marvin smiled to himself. For now, he had at least found something, which he was seeking and although he was surprised, Marvin continued to look through the yearbook and found additional pictures of Lionel during different school events along with many other prior students. From the pictures, he could see the racial mix of students was unevenly balanced with more African Americans and Hispanics than Anglos or Asians. This strengthened one of Marvin and Hope's theories of Lionel attending a school in an environment where he was racially outnumbered.

Then something popped into his mind, and he wondered why he hadn't thought of this before, Lionel's teachers. Only 15 years had passed, and Marvin was sure some of his teachers could possibly still be teaching at Compton High School. He then went back through the yearbook to list the names of teachers who may have had Lionel in their class as a student. Certainly, they would remember him. Class President in 1979 and eventually earning a medical degree. No teacher ever forgets those prize students.

With the information he had discovered, he felt there was nothing else to be learned by any additional search of the yearbooks. Although he had gained some relevant information, several unanswered questions still existed.

He gathered up the four volumes, arose from his chair and returned to the section where he had found the books and he carefully replaced them upon the shelf from which he had previously removed them.

Back at the information desk, he again thanked the clerk for her assistance and left the library. ~~He~~ Exited through the big doors, walked across the parking lot, and returned to his car. His original plan after visiting the library, was to head to the office of a local newspaper which had been in business since the early seventies.

Yet, from what he had found out about Lionel's high school days, maybe he should go there first. No, he said to himself. Let's stick with plan A.

He exited the parking lot and again following his maps, he headed downtown to the newspaper office to research the newspaper archives. He needed to see if he could find any mention of Lionel or his mother and in particular her domestic altercation issue with Jason Boone, he had learned about in last night's internet research.

33
CHAPTER

In an older building in the section of the city, which may have been the main shopping district, he found the newspaper office. Now, many of the buildings had boards covering their windows. A few open businesses remained but probably not a comfortable place to work.

He entered the office with a large sign above the door "The City of Compton Press Review" and as he walked into the office, he was met by an elderly woman who asked, "What can I do for you, sir?"

Marvin had to think for a moment and then said, "My name is Marvin Kushner, and I am a freelance writer doing some research about Compton in the late seventies and into the early eighties. I am hoping I can review some your newspaper archives for the period."

"Well, it sounds good but what specifically are you seeking?" the woman asked.

Marvin said, "Oh, just general events and news stories from the time which I can weave into my stories of the local area."

"Well, it is okay with me, but I hope you don't mind,

moving a stack of dusty boxes, I am sure you can find much information available which might be useful to you. By the way, how long do you think your looking will take?" asked the woman.

"Oh, I suspect no more than an hour or so if I can get to those dusty boxes easily. I am a quick reader," said Marvin.

"Well, follow me, sonny and I'll show you where the boxes are stored. Make sure you're done in an hour or so because I want to go home on time. This isn't the neighborhood to be staying out late." She then escorted him to a small storage room in the rear of the offices.

Marvin checked his watch and assured the woman he would be done very quickly as the woman lead him into a room with floor to ceiling shelving all laden with dusty boxes presumably filled with old newspapers. However, to Marvin's delight, each shelf was identified by year and each box was clearly identified with the month of publication.

The woman started to exit the room and turned to Marvin and said," It's all yours. Be sure to return the boxes to the shelves from where you took them and please put the newspapers back into the order the way they were in arranged in the box. If you need photocopies, bring the paper back to the office up front and I'll give you a copy. If not, I'll see you up front in one hour."

"Thanks, ma'am. I will do my best to be on time for you to leave."

Once the woman had left, Marvin wasted no time and immediately removed a box labeled May-July 1977. He carefully lifted out old edition's day by day, until he reached the one dated June 17, 1977. There on the front section was an article of the arrest of a Jason Boone for public drunkenness and fighting.

The story was very specific in every detail. Jason Boone had returned to his prior girlfriend's home very drunk and demanded to know why she had stopped seeing him. Apparently, she either gave him the wrong answer or he just wanted to punish her because he started to punch her. She was knocked to the ground and only was spared a further beating by aid of her son Lionel who had called the police and then Lionel began to hit Boone with a broomstick. Boone was very drunk and had a hard time maintaining his balance. Within a few minutes, the police had arrived and arrested him. The picture of Jason Boone on the front page was very clear and not so surprising to Marvin was the fact Jason Boone was African American but there was no picture of Lionel's mother.

Marvin felt there was not any additional information to be gained since he already knew the charges had been dropped by Lionel's mother, Mary Beth Viking. The other drunken charge did not mean much to him but may be useful in the future for Hope. He then put the newspapers back in the box in the proper order and placed the box back on the appropriate shelf. He walked to the front office, thanked the elderly woman, and left the newspaper office, twenty minutes earlier than he had promised.

"So far, so good," he said to himself as he entered his car to begin another part of his investigative quest.

His next stop, which he had added to his agenda, Compton High School. This could be a little trickier he thought to himself. What story is going to get me to a teacher who knows some details about Lionel as a person? He laid his head back onto the headrest in his car and sat still for about five minutes while a few scenarios drifted through his brain. Then suddenly, he knew exactly what he had to do.

He entered the school through the front door and following various directional signs, made his way through the corridor to the administration office. Opening the door, he was suddenly confronted by man who had been in the office working and who introduced himself as the Assistant Principal. "What can I do for you or maybe I should ask, who are you and why are you here?"

Marvin had pre-planned his answer and confidentially said, "Hi, my name is Marvin Kushner and I work for CMP, a major health care provider here in Southern California. We are doing a series of stories about some of our physicians and this school happens to have graduated one of our doctors in 1979. I believe he was Class President while he studied here. Lionel Viking is his name."

Well, said the assistant, "I have only been here five years, but I am sure somebody here will remember him. What sort of information are you seeking?"

"We publish a monthly newsletter, and we try to inform our patients about our doctors. We want them to know CMP doctors are regular people with backgrounds like most of the population. Not always stuffy white coated physicians but are individuals who grow up in average neighborhoods and went to regular public schools, such as this one."

Marvin continued, "By the way, I would think it also might be a good public relations story for the city and for your school. Students have a knack for identifying with successful alumni."

Well, I think it is great what CMP is doing Mr. Kushner and yes, I also believe it would be good for the school. You stay right here and let me quiz a couple of our long-term teachers. It was Lionel Viking, wasn't it?'

"Yes, Lionel Viking," said Marvin. He also smiled to himself and mused. Maybe I should be an actor or a sales representative.

Within a few minutes, the assistant returned with two middle-aged women. The Assistant Principal introduced them as Mrs. Sanchez and Mrs. Johnson. Both had taught at Compton High for many years, and both remembered Lionel Viking.

Marvin introduced himself and began his story. "It is a pleasure to meet you people. As I explained to the gentlemen, CMP, the large? Health provider located here in Southern California, is preparing to publish a series of articles on several of their physicians throughout California. One of these is Doctor Lionel Viking who currently is a Primary Care Physician in our Fountain Valley offices."

"Well, said, Mrs. Sanchez, I certainly am happy to hear about Lionel. I knew Lionel very well and I had him in a few of my classes during his time here. He was a very bright boy. A little introverted but bright and I just knew he would someday make a success of himself."

"Was he also one of your students, Mrs. Johnson?" asked Marvin.

"Yes, he was. I had him for Chemistry and Biology and as Mrs. Sanchez said, he was a bright boy. We're very proud of him. When I think back about him, for trouble he had at home, it was amazing he got so far in school."

"Why is that, asked Marvin?

"Well, I knew his mother and she was always running around with low life bums. Probably the reason for his being an introvert is because of his home life with no one to talk too. This left Lionel to fend for himself most of the time but a very determined kid and as you now know, he managed to do very well."

"Maria, do you remember the time when he tried to defend his mother from a beating by one of her ex-boyfriends?" "I think we have some more positive stories to tell about Lionel then about his mother. Frankly, as a student, he stayed focused on success. He performed well in a few science fairs and of course was Class President and was well liked by a lot of students. Unfortunately, he did not mix well with African American or Hispanic students. Maybe, because of his negative experiences with his mother and her friends."

"However, the end of the story is what counts. He made a success of himself and as Mrs. Johnson said, we are all proud of him."

Marvin had taken a few notes and thanked each of the teachers for their time and for the positive information. He then excused himself and left the building a little smarter than when he had entered it. Just like you are expected to do when you attend high school he thought.

Marvin sat in his car for a long time retracing his steps of his findings on this long day. He was very confident he had learned almost all he wanted to know about Doctor Viking from his high school days and beyond.

He removed his cellphone from the leather case and dialed Hope Moran's office. Her receptionist received the call, and he was immediately transferred to Hope.

Hope said, "Marvin, thanks for the call. What is new? Any further news about our doctor?

"Quite a bit," said Marvin. "I have had a very productive day and I am happy to say our doctor has led a very interesting life. Based upon what I have discovered so far, I believe you will have a challenging case fraught with twists and turns from high school to college and into his practice. I know you have had other challenges and I am sure you are up to the task for this case."

"Sounds very interesting, Marvin. When can we get together?"

"I am available any day this week," said Marvin.

They agreed to meet in two days at Hope's office.

The drive back to his home, on the freeway, proved to be slower and not as easy as his morning commute because of the afternoon rush hour traffic. It did not bother him as he had a good day and probably a gold medal day for Hope and her client.

I am sure, he thought, Hope will find this information useful and combined with the other information regarding Doctor Viking, she will agree to litigate the case.

34
CHAPTER

After returning home, Marvin had spent the rest of the evening organizing his findings. He knew Lionel did not like minorities, but he wondered how he could hold onto his personal dislikes for such a long period of time. After all, he is a doctor and doctors commit themselves to healing people, not killing them. He tried to understand the psychological enigma of Doctor Viking. It was difficult for him to understand how a highly educated person could harbor evil thoughts towards others based upon incidences, which had taken place in his life many years before.

Then again, he remembered his own personal experiences and what he had gone through as a drug addict, and he guessed not many people could understand why someone so educated and successful could become a drug user. Then he thought he would be better off not getting himself involved in trying to understand the psychological makeup of Lionel Viking. Perhaps it was a better decision to leave it to Hope and her legal team to determine what makes Lionel tick.

It was already quite late, and Marvin had given up his "what if" quest and he headed for the bedroom ready for a good night's rest.

It did not take him long to fall asleep after his busy day and he awoke after a sound night's sleep, took a shower, dressed, and went to the kitchen to get his first cup of coffee. While the coffee was brewing, he went downstairs to the lobby of his apartment house to get a newspaper from the stand in the lobby.

Sitting at his kitchen table, he was enjoying his coffee and newspaper. It was the first time in a few days he had a real opportunity to relax and get to learn about what else is happening in the world. The case had become obsessive and was consuming most of his time.

Around noontime, Marvin was ready to get back to the case and in about one hour, he had about completed his summary of his findings and reminded himself the car needed to have the oil changed. He drove the car to a Quick Lube shop, left his car and went to the restaurant across the street for lunch. He had just been served a cup of coffee when his cell phone rang. "Good afternoon, Hope."

"Hi, Marvin. I didn't disturb you, did I?"

"Nope, just sitting here with a cup of coffee. What can I do for you?"

"I am wondering if you are available to reschedule our tomorrow meeting and make it for today? I am almost sure; I am going to take the case against Doctor Viking based on your findings and our recent conversations."

"Sounds fine to me and I am glad you are considering taking the case. I can meet you in a couple of hours."

"That's good for me. See you then."

Marvin clicked off his phone and took another drink of his coffee. Meanwhile, the waitress stood by waiting for Marvin to order his lunch and to pour him his second cup of coffee.

He picked up his car after lunch and went to Hope's office just about on time for their meeting. The receptionist told Marvin; Hope would meet him in the conference room. He met Hope on his way to the conference room.

"Hello, Marvin, we now have some time so give me a summary of your findings in Compton and elsewhere and then give me your personal feelings about what you've learned about Doctor Viking."

"Hope, I believe the best starting point is when Lionel was in High School. Lionel was elected Class president in 1979 and based on discussions with two of his prior teachers, he was bright and focused but according to their comments, he didn't get along with the minorities at his school. His mother apparently was a loose woman and hung out with African Americans and Hispanics who more than likely abused her. One of his teacher's said Lionel was a constant witness to the many low life men in his mother's life. Somehow, he managed to succeed despite his mother and yet along the way, he failed to rid himself of his apparent hatred for all minorities."

"From high school, we move on to college and his leading a boycott against equal opportunity and then he goes to medical school and residency without any apparent negative occurrences. Upon completion of his residency, he is employed by CMP in LA where he has a minority incident; he is transferred to Irvine and another incident and again transferred."

"Now, we have James which is the third incident and the second one in Irvine."

"My God, what a track record and yet he is still on the payroll. Do you think he is a nut? Maybe a white supremacist or just a plain old bigot?"

"Psychologically, I don't know him so I can't make that call. The stuff I have been told is frightening for me as a former doctor and it could be worse for CMP's patients."

"Give me an educated guess whether he has psychological issues?"

"Yes, I firmly believe he does and based upon his profession, they are dangerous and life-threatening issues. Mr. Spencer is an example of what can happen when a doctor misdiagnoses a patient and particularly, when he does it as a premeditative act."

"Are you saying he intentionally overlooked Mr. Spencer's condition?"

"Absolutely. In my eyes he did because of two strong reasons. First, he obviously had the opportunity to do a correct diagnosis, and furthermore it is not his first incident of this type involving minorities. I believe in this case; it is akin to attempted murder or at least involuntary manslaughter."

"From a legal standpoint, you are probably correct and based upon all of what we know now, I am going to take the case involving Doctor Viking. However, keep in mind, we are taking this case to prove Doctor Viking was negligent in his care of Mr. Spencer. The court will quickly determine if criminal charges are warranted."

"I understand Hope."

"Tomorrow, I am asking the client to meet at my office where we can complete the details. This will be early in the morning and since you were going to be here, I want you to spend an hour or so with the client, James Spencer."

"Here is what I need you to find out from him. One, see if you can gather more information on his medical history. We will get better details when we obtain his chart from CMP. Try to learn more about his encounters with Doctor Viking. Quiz him on the status of his Melanoma and treatments. Get the names of his current doctors and do a background check on them. Lastly, try to learn a little more about his life history from a young teen until now."

"I'm glad you are taking this case and I am certainly interested in meeting James Spencer. I look forward to the meeting and perhaps, after tomorrow, we will have some more fuel to add to the fire."

35
CHAPTER

The next day, Marvin met with Hope again and she was very direct.

"Okay Marvin, James Spencer is now a client. We have all the necessary releases to gather evidence and by the way, the firm is taking this case on a contingency basis. James had an errand to run but should be back here in about one hour. This should give you some time to gather your thoughts. Ann will let you know when James returns to the office."

"Thanks Hope. I'll bring you up to date later."

Marvin spent the next hour putting his thoughts on paper and before he realized it, an hour had passed. Just then, the receptionist opened the door and advised Marvin; Mr. Spencer had returned from his errand and was now waiting in the reception area.

"Thanks Ann, tell him I'll be there in less than five minutes."

Marvin reassembled his notes and then went to meet James.

"Marvin it is sure a pleasure to meet you. Mrs. Moran told me about you. I am real happy Mrs. Moran agreed to take my case, as I really did need someone to go to bat for me. Now I can truly say I have Hope on my side."

Marvin smiled and said, "You're welcome, James and since we are just beginning, the firm will need some background information from you. As such, I want you to spend an hour or so with me. I do have a rather broad medical background. So, get yourself comfortable because you and I are going to get to know each other."

"James, let me start out by saying I am a familiar with your illness and I am also happy the firm is taking on your case. You will find Mrs. Moran is a true professional and you will be happy she is on your side. I was sorry to hear about your battle with Melanoma and I do have a good understanding about this cancer and what it takes to win the battle against it. Hence, I am going to ask you a few medically directed questions, which may or may not be usable for the legal team being assembled for this case. Are you ready to start?"

"If it means retribution, I am ready."

"We will take it one step at a time, James. Now tell me about when and where you first discovered or maybe felt something was wrong."

James discussed the entire history of the growth as he could remember it from the time, he first sensed it was something different on his arm, to his finding out about the cancerous growth and finally the details he knew about his current treatment.

"Now I would like you to tell me about your relationship with Doctor Viking. How long were you his patient and how did he treat you as a person? Can you remember some of his responses when you told him about the growth on your arm?

"I was his patient for about eight months, but I really did not have a doctor and patient relationship with him. Our time together was always very short, and I would estimate ten minutes on the high side but usually much less than ten minutes. He treated me okay and was pleasant. His responses to me when I advised him of the spot on my arm were usually some joking remarks, such as 'James everyone gets old age spots, or you had too much sun.' I know now he was just putting on an act for me. Maybe he is a fake doctor."

"James, did he ever really look at your arm as if he was doing an examination? Did he use magnification or a light to highlight the growth?"

"No, he never did any of those things. It was usually just a casual glance and then he was onto something else or on his way out of the examination room."

"That is interesting, James: Doctor Viking is a real doctor, but he did not treat you right. What you have told me will be helpful towards putting our case together. Now tell me who is your Primary Care Doctor now. Your dermatologist and your oncologist and where are you being treated?"

"Doctor Mancetti in Irvine is now my Primary Care Doctor, and he is really a good person. He is the one who spent time with me and who first provided me with an accurate diagnosis. Doctor Stuart is the dermatologist who confirmed the diagnosis and removed the growth. He is in Santa Ana near the airport. He is also very professional and very through. Lastly, I also meet my oncologist, Doctor Whetland, in Santa Ana. All of them keep me informed, answer my questions and are very supportive of me. I just wish Doctor Viking was as dedicated to me during my appointments as the doctors are now who are treating me."

"I am glad to hear you are now being treated properly but let us return to the subject of Doctor Viking. I am still curious about the amount of time the doctor spent with you each time you met with him, and can you tell me a little more about the conversations he had with you?"

"Lately, I have been thinking of all my encounters with the doctor. In all honesty, I doubt if any visit lasted more than five minutes but never more than ten minutes. Maybe, we can assume an average of seven minutes. It was, here I am and now I'm gone. For a while, I thought he might be paid as a piece part worker on a production line. Regarding conversations, they were always brief and when I mentioned my spot issue, he would sort of chuckle and tease me about getting old. Oh, regarding my cholesterol, he would always say I am doing great and keep up on your meds and you will be okay. Our conversations never really got to anything serious."

"So, you never had a real substantial medical conversation with him?"

"No, never."

"Thanks for the information. I'm making a note to myself to do some follow-up on the time aspect. Now let me ask you some more personal questions. First, give me a summary of your life from your early teens until now and I would like you to add any pertinent medical information you can remember which may not be contained in your current medical records. Any disease or illness possibly related to your current situation."

"Do we have enough time, Marvin?"

"We have as much time as you need, so start whenever you are ready."

36
CHAPTER

"To begin, I was born in 1935, in a small town, just south of Millinocket, Maine, sixty miles north of Bangor. My parents originally were from Eastern Canada and had immigrated south to the United States and like most folks during the depression period; they were in search of a better opportunity. My father was able to find work in a local shoe factory, not too far from our home.

"Our house was a small typical New England type cottage out in the countryside with only five rooms. My brother Bob was almost six years older, and we shared a small bedroom, which I later inherited when Bob left to attend college in Boston.

"My first recollection of Maine was the snow falling gently one late October morning and my dad awakening me to hurry to have breakfast, so we could go sleigh riding. Years later, I remembered the thrill of sitting on the same sleigh with its team of horses pulling us across a fresh base of snow on Farmer Clements' field. This ritual was to be repeated yearly and was still in vogue long after I left Maine for college and the city life.

"Farmer Clements, as he was known, was our closest neighbor. He was a gentle person who had also migrated from Canada some years earlier. He farmed about seven acres of rocky Maine soil growing enough food, mostly potatoes, for his family and some to sell. He also did some logging and maple syrup collecting in the spring. Nobody in the area had much money since the country was still recovering from the depression. They did have food and shelter and like all small American towns, our neighbors were good honest folks who shared their meager essentials.

"My parents were loving nurturing people who always stressed the importance of an education. Both mother and father spoke Canadian French, but they insisted Bob and I speak English and as such, both of us are bilingual.

"My father wished one of his children would become a lawyer or doctor, however, neither Bob nor I had any interest in those directions. We did however go to college and grow up to be law-abiding citizens and took our responsibility serious.

Both of us developed a sort of, "Maine stick to it" approach to problem solving. Mom's wish was only for us to be good people and to respect the rights of others, yet she also stressed, we should always defend those who were being wronged.

"The years drifted by and for me, it seemed to be a continuous program of starting school in the fall, harvest time, the first snow, sleigh rides, pond skating and then into spring. Then finally school let out for the summer and both Bob and I were expected to work. Half of what we earned went into a college fund, one quarter to Mom for help with the home costs as she called them and the balance we could use for our clothes and entertainment. I can still recollect the first pair of shoes I bought with my own money; Buster Browns. They stayed like new for a long time.

"The best source of income my brother and I had was helping farmer Clements sow his fields in the spring and then helping with the harvest in the fall. He had acquired a couple of Holsteins when I was in elementary school, and he taught me how to milk them. The Spencer family got free milk because of my labor and farmer Clement's kindness. Additionally, I got to play with farmer Clement's daughter Ruth, who became my best friend in the whole world.

"Ruth and I would sit for hours on her porch and try to figure out what we wanted to be when we grew up. She had an inquisitive mind and was always first to answer a question in school. Having a bit of mischief in her though. She liked to tease me at times about my shaggy hair, which seemed to grow in all directions. She once persuaded me to put a little lard on it to smooth it down and soon my head was covered with flies. She never forgot the story and years later after we were married, she did not hesitate to tell it; always ending up laughing as she did as a child.

"My school years seemed to fly by so fast and before I knew what was happening, I was a senior in high school. There were only 32 seniors graduating and Ruth and I shared top billing. We attended the prom together: me with my shaggy hair and Ruth with her frilly dress.

"Next was college. Bob finished at Boston College. He got there on a partial scholarship and became an accountant and then a CPA. He always had a head for figures."

Marvin said, "Well, so far it sounds like you had an interesting childhood, good neighbors and wonderful parents."

"Yes, I did. I wanted to be an engineer and my dad said I could repair anything and was exceptionally good at mathematics. So, off I went to attend Northeastern in Boston where they had a cooperative program which allowed me to work every other semester to earn money to pay my way through college.

"Meanwhile, Ruth had enrolled in a small teaching hospital in Bangor Maine studying to be a nurse. We would see each other about once or twice a month since it was only a couple of hours drive from Boston."

"Three years after I had begun my college education, the Korean War started. I was able to obtain a student deferment, which allowed me to avoid the draft while I remained in college and while the war continued. My dad reminded me to get an education first and then if I wanted to enlist, it would be my choice. Hence, my routine was much the same for almost six years."

"I would go to school one semester and work one semester. Some of the jobs I had were very easy. In my fourth year, I went to work for a computer company and was adopted by the Engineering Manager. He gave me hard assignments and forced me to practice everything I had been taught. Every now and then, he would pull me aside and give me a stern lecture about the necessity of being honest and hard working in your profession and men with integrity did not slack off. It was then I wondered if they would consider me for future employment since I was graduating in less than a year. To my surprise, the Engineering Manager, told me if I didn't come back, he would haunt me forever and then the company gave me the highest offer any student had previously received.

"In the meantime, Ruth had finished her nursing program and was working in a small hospital not far from both our homes. We had been talking about marriage and now I had landed this great job, I headed to Maine to propose. Both families were not surprised and were very happy for their children. After all, we had grown up together and both families had accepted each of us as just another one of their children. We planned a wedding for one month after I graduated, and we would then move to Boston where I had the job offer. Ruth could easily get a job in one of the many hospitals in the area. Unfortunately, though, now I had graduated, the Army had more of an interest in me than the computer company and they sent me a special delivery draft notice to prove it."

"Ruth and I decided to delay the wedding plans until after I had completed basic training at Fort Lee, Virginia where I suffered through 10 weeks of basic training. For some reason, the Army and I did not like each other but, because of my engineering degree, I was offered a commission and the chance to go to Radio School at Fort Benning, Georgia. I easily accepted both offers from the Army and then headed home to marry my childhood sweetheart and best friend.

"We honeymooned in a small town just outside of Atlanta and then it was back to school for me while Ruth managed to get a nursing job at Emory University. Because of the distance between Fort Benning and Atlanta, we could only see each other weekends and even then, both of us had studying to do. Not the romantic time we thought about, but we both felt our time would come soon enough."

"After graduating from Radio School, I was commissioned a Second Lieutenant in the Army. Unfortunately, the Korean War persisted, and I received orders for "duty beyond the seas," which, in plain English, meant I would soon be on way to Korea. I was given a five-day pass and told to report back to the base ready to leave immediately thereafter upon my return.

"Ruth took the message rather hard, but, understood that I didn't have much choice in the matter. We spent five days trying to catch up on all the romance we had tried to enjoy between her job and my studying. The days just seemed to disappear and before we knew what was happening, I was headed to Korea. Ruth had already decided to move back to Maine to be close to family and friends. It was a very sad time for the two of us."

"Korea was a complete culture shock for the boy from Maine and for the Army to put me in the middle of a war among people and ideologies which to me were totally alien. As an officer, I initially worked with a combat group in organizing their communications, but I was soon transferred to an elite communications group handling sensitive transmissions between Army headquarters in Korea and the Pentagon. I was only in Korea about one year when the war suddenly ended and happily, I received orders to report back to the USA for further instructions.

In the meantime, I was given a 30 day leave and immediately headed for Maine to my wife and family."

"Shortly after my arrival, Ruth and I headed, Down East as they say in Maine, to explore the beautiful Maine coastline. After my tour in Korea, the US was beautiful in all respects. This is especially true about the coast of Maine with its small towns and rocky inlets, where lobster traps and fishing boats present a colorful rustic setting. It was the first time that Ruth and I had opportunity to share ourselves with each other, without the uncertainty regarding our future together. We talked of starting a family and what I would like to do after being discharged from the Army. We spent moonlit nights walking together along the jetties listening to the gentle splash of the water upon the rocks and feeling the tenderness of each other. It was a very romantic time before we headed back towards Millinocket, sharing a glow only lovers know so well."

"My days of leave from the Army were soon up and again I had to leave Ruth and the people who meant so much to my life. I had orders to report to the Pentagon where I was to undergo additional communications training for the balance of my three-year tour. As it turned out, this training exposed me to a few commercial companies who let me know they would be interested in my skills should I decide to leave the Army. I had no second thoughts on this matter; for three days earlier Ruth had informed me we were going to be parents. From that moment on, I began to start counting the days until I would become a civilian. Not that I did not like the Army, as they had taught me a lot about myself and provided me the skills to allow me and my family a wonderful career and life. About four months later, I was released from the Army and headed home to decide on a future for the new Spencer family.

"One of the companies I had worked with while serving in the Pentagon was Windstep Electronics. They were a small but elite company based in Massachusetts specializing in sophisticated radar systems for both commercial and military applications. I contacted one of the engineers with whom I had developed a relationship and I was soon contacted by the company president. Within a few days, I was offered an engineering job basically working on the same systems I had worked on in both Korea and at the Pentagon. After discussing this with Ruth, I accepted the job. She was happy we could live in the Boston area, not too far from our families. We also realized we would be close to some of the finest medical facilities in the United States should Ruth desire to continue her education. In the fall of 1954, we moved to Burlington, Massachusetts, the city where we had put a small deposit down on a starter home."

"In February of that year, our daughter Jill was born and over the next five years, we added another girl and a boy to the family. I continued to work on advanced radar systems and gradually was promoted to more challenging assignments within the company. Ruth managed to stay home and raise our children. We enjoyed the usual family things and the years passed and were measured by graduations, birthdays, and anniversaries. We spent considerable time in Maine visiting our families and would spend at least two weeks a year on the Maine shore.

"My father died in 1963 followed a year later by Farmer Clements, Ruth's dad. Both our mothers passed within a couple of years after the death of their spouses."

"About the same time, Windstep Electronics bought an electronics company in California which would become Windstep Electronics, West.

Windstep Electronics had located their West Coast facility in Irvine, as did several other major electronic and medical equipment corporations. The attraction for them was UC Irvine, a university with a strong engineering school and excellent medical and biomedical research facilities.

I was appointed Vice president of Engineering of this expansion for Windstep. I received a sizable salary increase plus the usual relocation perks which were common in the emerging electronics businesses and thus Ruth and I and our three children found our way to Irvine California.

Lowering his eyes he said, "Ruth died almost three years ago from an errant blood clot. It wasn't too long after her death when I decided to retire. The rest of the story you already know."

Marvin asked, "How long were Ruth and you married, James?"

"Forty-two years. I knew her for almost sixty years and still miss her today. I am fortunate to have all my children and grandchildren in the area."

Marvin Thanked James for his time and for answering his questions so completely about his current medical situation and his personal life presentation. Marvin also noted that James appeared to be tired and as an ex-physician he knew this was the result of the treatments he was undergoing.

"Have you signed medical disclosure forms with Hope?"

"Yes," said James. She has told me the need to begin collecting information from several sources, but this would only be possible if I consented to a release of the information."

"Good, James because I intend to review your medical history in detail and specifically, the last year or so. I am sure some interesting tidbits will show up. Currently, I have no further questions to ask you. Do you have any for me?"

James thought for a moment and then asked, "What is a typical period for the entire legal process?"

"There is no standard time which can be quoted reasonably. It could be one year or much more dependent on how strongly the defendant wants to contest the charges."

"Marvin, I pray that somehow it moves along faster as the way I feel now, I honestly believe, I will be dead in one year or less."

With that gloomy assessment Marvin said, "Don't give up James. Think positively about being cured." He again thanked James for the meeting and wished him success with his treatments.

Before he left, he assured James that whether he was alive or dead, he would work hard towards fulfilling his wish for retribution.

37
CHAPTER

While James was busy meeting with Hope, Doctor Viking was sitting in his new office at CMP's Fountain Valley facility. He was still somewhat in shock because of having been transferred for the second time in his short career for misdiagnosing a patient. It wasn't because he felt he was being singled out for his lapses but rather he felt he had become a disappointment to himself and the medical profession.

The reason for the action taken by CMP for this recent episode involved a female Hispanic patient who chose to get a second opinion of her diagnosis by Doctor Viking from another doctor and this doctor had determined she had the onset of Type II Diabetes. Yet, her medical records showed no indication the woman had ever been questioned or tested for this condition. Beyond the lack of the diabetes determination, the woman also contended Doctor Viking was somewhat curt to her during her visits and she felt insulted by his actions and for what she interpreted as a lack of concern for her well-being.

As in the first instant of this type, Doctor Viking was only transferred, and a mild rebuke was entered into his personnel folder. CMP paid the woman a modest settlement fee without involving outside attorneys and the woman was apparently satisfied.

Lionel had committed himself to improving his behavior with minorities while assigned to the Irvine facility and in his mind; he was making good progress in his performance. Obviously, he went wrong with this patient. He knew however, he now had to double his efforts and had to stay constantly aware of his actions when meeting with minority patients. He committed himself to focus himself on their medical needs and not the color of their skin or their mangling of the English language. Again, the transfer provided him another opportunity to begin anew.

All the actions he was trying to institute to cause a behavioral change were admirable. Yet still, he had failed to recognize or confront any of his past actions. Neither he nor CMP were aware of the number of minorities Doctor Viking had seen and perhaps misdiagnosed. His previous actions were of the past and he never thought of previous patients he might have wronged. Likewise, CMP never gave any further thought to his two blemishes.

Lionel remembered his meeting with the Director of Residency at LA County Hospital, now almost three years ago and how he was reprimanded and told to improve his behavior or to leave Medicine. However, he had been able to change his behavior and became a model doctor. I did it successfully once he thought and I am perfectly capable of doing it again, he told himself.

Forgetting the past and moving into the future while modifying his behavior became his mantra for his new assignment at Fountain Valley. Tomorrow will be the first of day of the new Doctor Viking, he promised himself subconsciously.

38
CHAPTER

After Hope had met with James, she convened a meeting with one of her staff attorneys to draft the formal complaint for filing with the Superior Court in Santa Ana California which had jurisdiction over this case. It is customary to have the formal complaint transmitted to the Superior Court and then the court formally serves the complaint to the defendants. It is the first notice to the defendants of their being confronted with a legal action.

The plaintiff would be James Mark Spencer and the first defendant would be Lionel P. Viking, Doctor of Medicine. Added to the defendant list would be Coastal Medical Practitioners a.k.a. CMP of Irvine, California and their parent corporation, PAC-Health Inc., headquartered in San Francisco.

Hope told the staff attorney the details and proper addresses and locations of the defendants could be obtained from her legal assistant but her main concern now was preparing the draft rapidly so it could be properly filed with the court by the end of the week.

She had previously dictated a summary of the charges to be specified on the complaint and she gave the staff attorney the following copy:

Defendant A: Lionel P. Viking MD

Gross negligence according to Cacival Code 1812.10 et al

In that Dr. Viking failed to meet established standards and provide adequate care and diagnosis to the plaintiff on at least two or more occasions and therefore became negligent under the rules and standards established by the Medical Board of California. Such negligence and misdiagnosis resulted in the plaintiff to later be diagnosed with Stage III Melanoma, confirmed to be localized, which has resulted in significant pain and suffering for the patient and could very well result in future death to the plaintiff.

Additionally, there are concerns and information concerning the said defendant violated said plaintiff's civil rights and therefore the afore stated negligence could be considered premeditated under California code.

Defendant B: Coastal Medical Practitioners, AKA CMP, A California Corporation Defendant A is gainfully employed by Defendant B and as such CMP is also a party to negligence in overseeing the activities of Defendant A. CMP knew specifically Defendant A had difficulties on more than one occasion as noted by their transmission of data regarding Defendant A to the California Medical Board and as such, CMP had full knowledge of Defendant A's history involving minorities and yet CMP failed to provide adequate protection for the minority patients of Defendant A and to enforce CMP directives defining patient physician relationships.

Defendant C: Pac-Health Inc., A California Corporation Pac-Health Inc. is the parent corporation of Defendant B and as such share's individual and joint responsibility for the practices of Defendant A and Defendant B.

Hope than directed the staff attorney to begin preparing the draft. She then directed to be sure to include all relevant California legal code information plus the recommended compensation for non-economic damages of two hundred and fifty thousand dollars, attorney and other legal fees and possible punitive damages in the amount of three million dollars.

About the time that Hope had finished her meeting with the staff attorney, Marvin had escorted Jim back to the reception area and said his good-byes to him. He then returned to the conference room to try to put much of what he now knew about this case into perspective. While he was thinking about the case, Hope returned to the room to have further discussion with Marvin about his meeting with James.

"This is not going to be an easy case for me," said Marvin. "James is a fine gentleman, served his country as an officer in Korea and the Pentagon. He has worked at the highest levels of management for a major US corporation. He played by all the rules and perhaps he is now dying because a doctor was having fun playing by a set of evil rules."

"I know this is difficult for you, Marvin but, you and I must operate unemotionally and arm's length from James. I understand your anger, but this firm has a case to prosecute, and we must operate within the rules of the court and to present the honest facts before the court. We must let the system work to balance the scales of justice."

"It is strange, when I was practicing medicine, I also had to suppress my emotions so I could deal intelligently and professionally using my trained skills to serve my patients with a high standard of care. But we are all human and there are times when it is difficult to contain your emotions. It is during those times; I just must let off a burst of steam and then it's time to move on."

"Is now the time?"

"The steam has been let off and is now dissipating."

"Good let's summarize what we have now. Let's start with James."

Marvin provided Hope a summary of James' life based on the interview. He reiterated James was highly educated and has been a hard worker most of his life and was only beginning to enjoy his retirement after losing his wife of many years. His failing, if he had one, was trusting a medical professional as he had trusted other professionals during his very successful career as a top-notch design engineer and executive.

"Very well stated Marvin. Here is what I have about Doctor Viking. He is more than likely a racist and probably has been from his early teens. He treats minorities as if they were vermin and then slithers away like a snake in deep grass. Why he has not been stopped by CMP after the second incident is a mystery to me because I know they have been a well-regarded provider of medical services to the public and a successful corporation. They certainly do not want this kind of notoriety and realistically, this could be major corporate blunder for them. They will think long and hard about their failure to act on Doctor Vikings behavior after all the costs are finally added up."

Hope continued, "The facts we have today clearly indicate Doctor Viking can be charged with discrimination against James. This information will eventually be turned over to the district attorney's office for them to litigate. Clearly, he was negligent and failed to provide reasonable care not because he wasn't qualified but only because James's race is African American. The delayed diagnosis could very well result in being fatal to James."

"Hope, it appears to me, we now have a good starting argument about Doctor Viking, I believe it is time to obtain further details from James' current doctors. We have his authorization to release his complete medical records. I want to review them line-by-line to see what I can add to the information we have thus far. I believe there maybe additional clues of James' illness perhaps overlooked by Doctor Viking because of his color blindness. Anything of substance would be the final nail in the coffin for the doctor. With your permission, I would like to start the search right away."

"I agree. We have enough evidence to file the complaint with the Superior Court. So, begin post haste because we can always amend the complaint very quickly. There is also the possibility of one of his current doctors may also be emotionally involved and has strong negative feelings for Doctor Viking."

"I will start immediately tomorrow morning. My thoughts mirror yours because I also feel one of his doctors or perhaps all of them, will eventually provide some damaging information against Doctor Viking."

Marvin then advised Hope, he would be in the office most of the week and he should be able to keep her updated as to his findings.

Hope thanked him, left the conference room, and headed for her office. Unfortunately, she knew, her thoughts would soon stray back to her newest case, James Spencer versus Doctor Lionel P. Viking et al.

Meanwhile, Marvin continued to review the history of James's medical problems, but he knew it would be better to have his history while he was under the care of CMP in front of him. He checked with the receptionist to get a copy of James agreement to release medical data concerning him to third parties. He quickly received a copy and wrote a formal letter to CMP requesting the complete medical records for James Mark Spencer. When he had finished the letter, he faxed the letter and release document signed by James to CMP offices in Irvine.

It was now almost seven thirty at night and he decided it was time to call it a day. He left the office, but his mind was still fixated on Doctor Viking and the damage he had created to his unsuspecting patient.

39 CHAPTER

The next day, Marvin arrived at the legal offices within a few minutes of the office opening. He immediately went to his office and to his surprise there was a large stack of documents placed in the center of his desk. He sat down and selected the top document to determine what it was regarding. To add to his surprise, a handwritten note paper clipped on top of the stack of papers, from Doctor Mancetti.

Dear Marvin,

> You may not recall but we met some years ago at a medical conference for ER practices in San Diego. I understand your connection to the patient and if there is any further information I can provide you, please feel free to contact me.
>
> Regards
> Bob Mancetti MD

Marvin was sort of astonished on two counts. First, having received James's medical history so rapidly and second, the personal note from Doctor Mancetti. As he was about to scan through the stack of documents on his desk, Hope walked into his office.

"Good morning, Marvin."

"Morning, Hope. I was just beginning to review the medical history documents of James sent to me by CMP. They certainly acted fast to my request and interestingly Doctor Mancetti, James' assigned physician, sent me a personal handwritten note telling me to contact him should I need additional information. It seems strange, because he must know the reason for my request of James' information is to use the medical records for legal use!"

"Marvin, I am glad to know the doctor is willing to help you but please have no further contact with Doctor Mancetti or any other medical provider employed or contracted with CMP if it regards James. This is a big no-no and if CMP's attorneys were to discover a personal relationship, it would be troublesome for our case to say the least."

"I understand, Hope and you can be assured, I will stay far away from CMP and their staff. It did occur to me the good doctor has perhaps discovered a bad doctor and like myself, he also finds it revolting."

"I hear you, but you must stick to the rules of the game, and it means no contacts of a personal nature."

"The reason I came to your office is to let you know that the complaint draft is being prepared. It is my objective to have it delivered to the court by the end of this week. Whenever it is available, I plan on distributing the draft to the staff involved in this case, which includes you. It will give you the opportunity to review the charges and requested damages. In addition, I would like your assessment after you review James' medical record and particularly if you find some interesting bits of data in the medical history."

"Thanks, Hope, I assume it will take me about three or four hours to thoroughly review and digest the client information I have received this morning."

Hope then left Marvin's office and he then began to sort through the large stack of papers in front of him.

40
CHAPTER

Having been a trained physician, Marvin understood both the simplicity and complexity of patient histories. The entire process of collecting the data for a specific patient is to maintain as complete record of all medical aspects, from birth until death, relating to the patient. It is intended to help medical caregivers of all types who may be engaged with the patient to better understand the patient. The medical history also serves as a useful tool for future diagnosis of a disease or illness, which maybe contracted by the patient.

To keep the history updated and relevant, a practitioner typically asks a variety of questions to obtain information about the patient:

Identification and demographics: name, age, height, and weight.

The chief complaint at the time of each encounter with the medical practitioner, i.e., the major health problem or concern and at the time of the encounter.

History of the present illness including details about the complaints presented by the patient.

Past medical history including major illnesses, any previous surgery and operations and notes from surgeons, any current ongoing illness, etc.

Review of systems, which is a systematic questioning about different organ systems of the patient.

Family history and diseases especially those relevant to the patient's chief complaint. Typically, the family history lists the health status of immediate family members as well as their causes of death if known. It may also list diseases common in the family or found only in one sex or the other.

Childhood diseases

Social history including living arrangements, occupation, marital status, number of children, drug use (including tobacco, alcohol, other recreational drug use), recent foreign travel, and exposure to environmental pathogens through recreational activities or pets.

Regular and acute medications including those prescribed by doctors, and others obtained over the counter or alternative medicine being used by the patient.

Allergies to medications, food, latex, shellfish, and other environmental factors.

Marvin knew although the history process was very through, the introduction of computers into the medical field meant patient records were becoming more detailed and easier to maintain and distribute to caregivers. Medical histories stored online were now readily available instantly for those with the need to know.

Although James's entire history going back many years was of interest to him, Marvin's main interest was in the previous year and thus he sifted through the papers until he reached a date of December 1994.

It was on this date, the 29 of December; James had an appointment with Doctor Viking for a normal six-month checkup. The records clearly indicated the doctor performed a simple exam and James did not have any specific claim of illness although it was noted, he did point out the spot to Doctor Viking. James had told him in their recent meeting Doctor Viking teased him about getting older and about age spots periodically making their presence known to everyone as they age. The doctor reminded James to continue his cholesterol medication and his exercise program. All other aspects of the appointment were normal.

In early May, James had another appointment to review the results of a blood panel, which had been collected one week before from James. He was first seen by the receiving nurse who checked his weight and temperature measurements and then his blood pressure. All appeared to be normal. Doctor Viking noted all of James's blood work was also normal and his overall cholesterol had improved.

It was also noted that James had again asked the doctor about the spot on his arm and told him it was itching. The doctor took a cursory look at the spot and told James he would write a prescription for him prescribing an ointment containing one percent Hydrocortisone to relieve the itching. The record showed James was advised to use the ointment twice daily and to also apply a sunscreen 30 SPF or higher whenever he went outdoors. Lastly the doctor advised him to wear long sleeve shirts outside the home and to avoid excessive exposure to the sun.

There was one final notation, which appeared worrisome for Marvin. It read, "During the next scheduled visit, check for possible skin cancer if the growth still exists."

Marvin wondered about such a strange notation for a doctor to make especially when the patient is complaining about a medical issue and a look by the doctor would have taken less than ten minutes. Marvin felt that Doctor Viking had the opportunity to redeem himself by performing additional tests but instead passed up the opportunity. But, why and why the incriminating note? He is somewhat of a Doctor Jekyll and a Doctor Hyde thought Marvin.

The next meeting with the medical staff was about four weeks later when James made an appointment specifically to discuss the spot and the fact that James sensed the spot was growing larger and perhaps changing color.

He had gone through the usual pre-examination tests by the nurse and was finally seen by Doctor Mancetti. This doctor listened to the concerns of James and performed an in-depth examination of the affected area. His entries were as follows:

Patient is an African American male aged 61 and in relatively good health. He has complained about a spot on the exterior of his right forearm on at least two previous encounters while a patient of CMP during the previous six months.

The initial examination by myself using high-density lighting and magnification revealed a growth located on the exterior of his right forearm approximately three inches below the elbow. The growth was slightly raised, one to two millimeters in height with a serrated edge and the overall size of approximately eight to ten millimeters in diameter. Coloration was a faded brown with two small black spots approximately in the center of the growth.

I advised the patient in my opinion; he should immediately be referred to a dermatologist and I would be glad to make the necessary arrangements for him. The patient agreed to see a specialist and I arranged an appointment for the next day with Doctor Stuart, CMP's resident dermatologist.

I also advised the patient to discontinue all skin medications he might be using but to continue with sunscreen applications and the wearing of long sleeve shirts while exposed to sunlight.

I told him I would be in contact with Doctor Stuart to follow the progress of his complaint.

Lastly, I asked the patient if he had any additional complaints. The patient's response was negative.

Marvin was glad that Doctor Mancetti had been so thorough in his examination and documentation but unhappy about the fact Doctor Viking had failed not once but twice to properly diagnose the patient. He scribbled a note to himself to tell Hope of this oversight.

Marvin began to read the report of Doctor Stuart posted one day later.

His examination was like Doctor Mancetti's but also included removal of the growth with clear directions to analyze the biopsy from the removed section.

He ended his entries into the report with the following notations:

a. Patient has obvious melanoma growth perhaps in advanced stages.
b. Patient complained of this growth to a CMP primary care physician on at least two previous occasions before any further detailed examination or testing was performed by CMP medical staff.
c. Patient advised the biopsy results would be available in four to five days and this office would contact him for a follow-up appointment.
d. The patient also advised to apply fresh bandages daily for the first three days after surgery and to take Tylenol for pain.
e. The patient advised to call our office should excess redness or pain occur in the surgery area.
f. The patient also advised Doctor Mancetti would receive information of the biopsy results.
g. The patient stayed in the examination room until he had recovered from sedation and then his daughter drove him home.

The thorough findings by Doctor Stuart more than likely disturbed the doctor, James, and his daughter.

Marvin sat back in his chair for a few moments, thinking about what he had read in the history. He felt there's a gap missing in James's history. "I know something is not right," he said to himself. What? Family history! There is no family history in the records. He sat up in his chair and reached for the telephone to call James.

"James, Marvin here. How are you doing today?"

"Hello, Marvin. Today, I feel worse than I have in a couple of weeks. Interesting I feel a lot weaker. Maybe my treatments are starting to rid me of this terrible weight I carry but in turn they are making me very ill."

"I am sorry to hear about your condition, James. It is one of the downsides of your treatments. Let us hope the treatments are doing their job and you begin to see some improvement. The reason for my call is I did not find any references to your family history in your medical records. Did anyone ever ask you about your immediate family regarding diseases, illnesses, causes of death?"

"From what I can recall, nobody ever asked about my family."

"Okay, let me ask you this. Are you aware of any family member on your mother or father's side having skin problems or any kind of cancer? Uncles, aunts, or cousins?"

"No, I do not know. But I can call my brother Bob who is six years older and maybe he knows more about the family. If I can reach him, I should be able to call you back in less than one hour."

"Thanks, James. I will wait to hear from you."

Marvin went back to his reading the medical history and jotting notes as he read. Within twenty minutes James had called him back and confirmed, one of his uncles on his father's side had died in Canada from skin cancer. His death was more than 60 years ago and James' brother Bob being twelve at the time remembered very little about it. What type of cancer caused the uncle to die was also unknown.

Marvin thanked James for the information and realized that 60 years ago, not much was known about any kind of cancer but still, it would have been helpful to have it in his history.

He returned to his study of the records and thought, another miss for Doctor Viking and an obvious oversight, which should have been in

James' records. When he almost completed his review, he wondered how many more oversights against minorities did Doctor Viking knowingly omit in his practice?

41
CHAPTER

As Hope promised, the draft complaint was distributed about mid-afternoon to the responsible staff attorneys and investigators to read, edit, add, or amend or to add additional commentary. The document would then be revised and again distributed to the staff for final approval.

Once approved by the firm, the Superior Court in Santa Ana, being the relative court, would receive the complaint for filing. This is the court, which had been designated as the responsible court for civil wrongs involving medical malpractice complaints within the Orange County jurisdiction.

Marvin had seen these complaint forms on many occasions during his tenure with Hope's firm. He always thought the legal practice was not too much different from the medical practice. They both followed very precise rules, which clearly defined right from wrong.

He slowly leafed through the various pages before returning to page one. Now he began to slowly read the draft complaint in its entirety, detail by detail.

Registered Attorney:
Hope Moran
17201 Orange Grove Towers
Suite 1472
Irvine CA. 92606
State Bar Number H4269001MM
Telephone:(949) 666-3444
Attorney for: James M. Spencer

Formal Complaint Form CA 92716 Rev 12, 1991

To be submitted to the Clerk of Courts
within the appropriate jurisdiction

Superior Court of the State of California County of Orange

Plaintiff: James M. Spencer	CASE No: OCSCC MM42119075
3378 Red Hawk Road	
Irvine, CA. 92655	Complaint for Negligence
DEFENDANT(S) NAMES	Medical Malpractice
Lionel P. Viking M.D. Defendant A	
C/O CMP	
2700 Barranca Parkway	
Irvine CA. 92656	
Coastal Medical Practitioners (CMP) Defendant B	
2700 Barranca Parkway	
Irvine, CA. 92655	

Pac-Health, INC.	
Defendant C	
44404 State Street Place	
San Francisco, CA. 94102	

The plaintiff complains about causation of action and alleges as follows:

1. Plaintiff, James M. Spencer is an individual and is now, and at all times mentioned in this complaint, a resident of Orange County, California.
2. Defendant A, Lionel P. Viking M.D., is now, and at all times mentioned in this complaint, gainfully employed by the codefendant's corporations organized and existing under the laws of the state of California with its place of business in Orange County, California. Additionally, Lionel P. Viking is a licensed physician practicing under the jurisdiction of the Medical Board of California established by and existing under the laws of the State of California.
3. Defendant B, Coastal Medical Practitioners aka CMP, is now and at all times mentioned in this complaint, a corporation organized and existing under the laws of the State of California.
4. Defendant C, Pac-Health, INC., is now and at all times mentioned in this complaint, a corporation organized and existing under the laws of the State of California and is the parent corporation of CMP.
5. On or about December 29,1994, Lionel P. Viking, M.D., provided medical services while under the employment of CMP to James Spencer as a normal biannual checkup.
6. During the Plaintiff's encounter with defendant A, Plaintiff informed the defendant of the spot on his arm and defendant casually dismissed the complaint as noted in the plaintiff's medical records.
7. In early May 1995, Plaintiff again met with defendant A for results of various blood tests and again informed defendant A of his concern about the subject spot. Plaintiff was advised by defendant A not to be concerned as the spot was most likely due to age or excessive sun exposure. Plaintiff was given a prescription to relieve itching and sent home. All the above is also noted in Plaintiff's medical records.
8. In all encounters with the Plaintiff, Defendant A had the opportunity to provide a reasonable diagnosis but for reasons yet to be exposed, he acted as a wrongdoer and failed to perform to established standards of care.

9. In June 1995, Plaintiff became alarmed the medication prescribed by Defendant A not being effective and the subject spot continued growing and possibly changing color. He then arranged an appointment to again state his complaint with the doctor.
10. On or about June 16, 1995, at the time of his appointment, Plaintiff was advised his case and care would be the responsibility of a new primary care physician as Defendant A had been transferred to another CMP facility.
11. On or about June 16, 1995, plaintiff was examined by his newly assigned physician, Robert S. Mancetti, M.D. who recognized the seriousness of the growth on Plaintiff's arm. This physician was able to arrange an appointment with the Staff Dermatologist also under the employ of CMP to confirm his diagnosis. All of this is noted in Plaintiff's medical history.
12. On or about June 17, plaintiff was examined by Peter N. Stuart, M.D., Staff Dermatologist for CMP at the Santa Ana offices. Doctor Stuart confirmed the seriousness of the growth on the plaintiff's arm and performed an incision to remove the growth and have the remains studied and analyzed for type of cancer.
13. On or about June 28,1995, Plaintiff was informed of his diagnosis by Peter N. Stuart, M.D., whereby he learned he had an advanced stage of Melanoma.
14. Plaintiff further learned he would have to undergo various treatment options to continue his life.
15. All of this occurred as a direct result of negligence and the lack of medical care to known and accepted standards by Defendant A and his Joint Tortfeastors, Defendants B and C.
16. The result of this known negligence has caused Plaintiff to suffer physically and emotionally in the past and will continue to do so into the future.

Count 1 Negligence - Medical Malpractice

The Plaintiff re-alleges and incorporates by reference herein the allegations contained in paragraphs 1 - 16 above that Defendants A, Lionel P. Viking, M.D., Defendant B and Defendant C were negligent and did not apply known and accepted standards of care to Plaintiff. This negligence by all Defendants resulted in a lengthy delay in the appropriate diagnosis and has caused Plaintiff much emotional and physical harm.

Wherefore: The Plaintiff charges damages against Lionel P. Viking, M.D. and Defendants B and C in the amount to be determined at trial, plus costs and for any further relief this Honorable Court determines necessary and appropriate.

Respectfully Submitted,
Hope Moran, LLC

42
CHAPTER

After Marvin had completed his reading of the complaint, he began to compare his notes and observations versus the complaint lying upon his desk. Some of the legal terms used in the complaint Marvin did not understand. Hence,

He went online to get legal definitions for some of the words.

"Causation" he learned was a key component to establish liability in both criminal and civil law. In this case, he assumed it was the lack of standard care not being provided to James by Doctor Viking.

"A wrongdoer" seemed obvious and he discovered it was an individual who committed a wrongful act that injures another and for which the law provides a legal right to seek relief such as punitive damages or other damages against a defendant in a civil tort case.

The first two, he had a clue as to their legal definition but for the next one, "Joint Tortfeastors", he seemed clueless but quickly found the definition on one of the Internet dictionary sites. He had to read the definition a couple of times before he got the grasp of what it meant. "Joint Tortfeastors" is defined as two or more persons whose negligence in a single accident or event causes damages to another person. In many cases the joint Tortfeastors are jointly and severally liable for the damages, meaning any of them can be responsible to pay the entire amount, no matter how unequal the negligence belongs to each party.

In this case, he felt both Doctor Viking and CMP should share the liability for negligence. He did not know how Pac-Health would be treated but they are the parent corporation of CMP. However, he knew this should not be his concern. His responsibility required him to ensure the occurrence of medical negligence was clearly defined beyond a reasonable doubt.

He had further legal questions needing clarification and so he dialed Hope's office looking for answers, "Hope, Marvin here. Are you busy now as I need some legal clarifications."

"Okay, Marvin. I have time. What do you need?"

"Well, I note that the first charge on the complaint is for negligence about the standard of care. I was wondering if this also includes failure to include relevant information in the patient's medical records and failure to do additional testing when the record shows some knowledge of the patient's complaint. Is this considered an all-encompassing charge?"

"Typically, the initial complaint is limited to information which is 100 percent proof without any doubts or concerns the negligence was committed. There always will be amended complaints by us and counter complaints by the defendants.

Knowing this, our first objective is to get the complaint filed and then to really get to the nitty-gritty as the case moves ahead."

Hope continued, "Remember, we still have a long time, possibly nine months to one year before we ever get to stand before a judge and jury. The depositions of the defendants will possibly reveal other charges, which today, are totally unknown to us. Therefore, we wait to learn more and then we amend the complaint to include the newer allegations."

"Got it, Hope. Considering the notations by Doctors Mancetti and Stuart in the medical records, I am sure we will uncover additional charges during the depositions."

"I am glad you brought that up Marvin because sometime next week we need must sit down and begin pinpointing how, when and who we want to depose of the various defendants. We also need to start thinking about consultants and expert witnesses and schedule some time to conduct interviews with them. What I would like you to do the balance of this week is gather some info on all CMP doctors directly involved in this case. Additionally, draw up a list of possible medical consultants and expert witnesses specializing in primary care and skin cancers."

"OK, I will start tomorrow. I also think it may be important I do some investigating on how Doctor Viking is treating minorities now. For example, how long does he spend with a white patient versus a minority."

"Good idea, Marvin. When the complaint is filed and acknowledged by the defendants, we will begin to issue summons to CMP for various records regarding Doctor Viking's patients of every color. Some of these may make excellent witnesses for our side and I am sure they have some interesting stories to tell. In the meantime, do some undercover work at the Fountain Valley offices and try to assess how long every patient gets to see a doctor and this will establish some baseline information for us."

"Sounds like we are going to be busy for a few weeks or is it months?"

"No telling. If we find a bombshell early in the process, there should be a settlement, which typically happens, in 97 percent of all medically related cases. If the evidence we have now is all we can get, then it could last one or two years or more. Every case is different, and it will boil down to dollars for the defendants and for us. For our case, I am confident they will either pay now or take the chance of paying a lot more later."

"An interesting shell game." asked Marvin.

"Not really, because all of us, plaintiff, or defendant, must follow the laws as they are written. Our firm chases those who step outside of the law, and I use the leverage to try to make it right for my clients who were harmed. Meanwhile the defendants know they have broken the law but are trying to minimize the cost of dollars, reputation, etc. for their client."

"I'm still learning, Hope and I am fascinated by all of it. My objective is to be able to contribute to the firm and into this case with my limited knowledge."

"You are doing well, Marvin. As Socrates once said, "With age comes wisdom."

"Thanks for all the information, Hope. I am beginning to feel older already. We will talk again soon."

Marvin thought for a few minutes about everything that Hope had just told him and slowly he began to see the big picture of the legal world. He made a few notes on his to-do list and then returned to the reading of the complaint.

Considering his conversation with Hope, he did not have anything to add at this time. He initialed the draft copy, picked it up and walked to the reception area and returned the draft complaint to the receptionist to pass to whoever was preparing the revisions.

Returning to his office, Marvin said out loud, "James, I am working for you, buddy and today we took one more step towards retribution."

43 CHAPTER

There was a well-established documented procedure at CMP whenever there was a request for the transmission of a patient's medical records. To begin, the procedure required verification of the patient's authorization of the request before the records could be transmitted to the requesting party.

Then, any request for patient records to the medical or administrative staff had to be immediately followed with documented notification to CMP's internal security. The supervisor of the Security Department had to review the request and if the requestor of the patient's history file was a legal firm, the security department was required to provide a report to the internal Legal Department of CMP.

Again, per procedure, the internal legal staff noting a potential legal issue had to formally notify the outside counsel of Smitherson, Brunch and Fogel with complete details of the patient including his current medical status along with other relevant information.

The same day the medical records of James Spencer were sent to Hope Moran's legal firm, Ted Smitherson, one of the principal partners in the firm representing CMP, had received a copy of the file along with other information per the accepted procedures in force at CMP.

Ted had represented CMP for many years handling both their corporate legal needs and medical malpractice defense. Anything provided to him from CMP such as a patient's history meant concerns of legal action being taken against CMP. He immediately began to review the patient history and details. Although no formal complaint had been received from the court for this patient, experience had taught him when a request was made for a patient's medical history from a legal firm; a lawsuit was not very far behind.

He noted the name of the doctors who were directly involved with the patient, and he reread Doctor Mancetti's comments twice regarding the examination of the patient James Spencer. It was obvious to Smitherson the first doctor mentioned, Doctor Viking, would be the defendant and the charge would be for negligence, perhaps due to a failed diagnosis. From Smitherson's perspective, it appeared to be a "He said, she said" type of case and his initial reaction was the patient had a reasonable chance of being cured. Hence, it should be a relatively easy case with minimal cost to CMP, outside of the usual legal expenses.

Ted Smitherson had never been advised concerning Doctor Viking's previous history and the information of his being the leading character in two settlements of negligence and mistreatment of minorities while at CMP.

His firm had not handled these cases as the in-house attorneys at CMP quickly settled them. It was through an oversight or laxity by CMP internal legal team to not notify the outside counsel of Doctor Viking's previous behavior. Ted Smitherson also did not know, both settled cases involved minorities.

After having read the patient's history, he had his secretary make additional copies. Ted Smitherson then summoned two staff attorneys to his office and gave each of the staff members a copy.

"Gentlemen, please begin to familiarize yourselves with the information I have just given to you transmitted to me by CMP. From experience, I suspect we will see a complaint from the Superior Court regarding this matter within a few days. CMP is a long-established client, and our firm must respond with a cross complaint in a very timely manner."

"My own take on the matter is the case does not appear to be very complex on the surface. Yes, after you read, the details, there is a hint of negligence by the doctor, but I believe there is also some liability by the patient. Hence, some sort of compromise should be able to be reached without costs being unreasonable. Anyway, both of you review the details and then give me some comments and opinions regarding your impressions of the case. Then, we should be well prepared when the complaint comes our way."

Meanwhile within the in-house legal department of CMP, one of the attorneys noted Doctor Viking had been involved in another case. He thought, when are they going to put some reins on this guy. Alternatively, maybe it is best I just leave it to the Director of Physicians to make the call regarding Doctor Viking, since the other two settlements were relatively minor infractions and cost CMP very little.

More than a week later, the formal complaint from the Superior Court was received by CMP and per procedure was immediately passed to outside counsel. The charges were about what all the in-house attorneys at CMP and Smitherson, Brunch and Fogel were expecting. Legally, all the I's have been dotted and the T's crossed. The battle lines had been drawn. CMP versus Spencer was now a case.

44
CHAPTER

The day after CMP had been served with the complaint, Hope Moran's firm also received notification the complaint had been legally served upon each of the defendants. Hope knew, the next move would be by the legal firm representing the defendants, which per California law, allows them 30 days to provide an answer. She correctly assumed her firm would be receiving a counter complaint from Smitherson, Brunch and Fogel within two to three weeks, which she knew represented CMP for most of their legal requirements.

As part of his things to do list, Marvin had traveled to the Fountain Valley and Irvine offices of CMP. He sat in the waiting room for over one hour at each facility as if waiting for a patient he had brought to the offices for an appointment to see a doctor.

He kept time of the average visit for each patient from the time they were escorted into the examination area until they returned to the reception area. He was able to record the entry and exit of eleven patients, of which three were clearly identified as patients for Doctor Viking.

The average visit time was twenty-two minutes for all eleven patients including three minority patients. Doctor Viking saw only one minority patient and the patient's visit lasted only eight minutes. Doctor Viking's white patients averaged just over twenty minutes.

From the Fountain Valley Facility, Marvin drove to the Irvine facility and using the same methodology, recorded the time of a patient entering to see the doctor and the time of the patient exiting after the visit. In Irvine, the average visit time equaled approximately 18 minutes regardless of ethnicity.

Marvin appeared happy with the results he observed, and they corresponded very well with recent medical surveys showing the time spent with primary care doctors averaged 21 minutes throughout the United States.

He next started on his due diligence and background review of Doctor Mancetti, Doctor Whetland and Doctor Stuart. His search revealed they were all very experienced physicians with clean histories per the California Board of Medicine and legally, none of them had ever been engaged as a defendant in a medical malpractice situation.

Doctor Stuart was a Fellow of the American Academy of Dermatology and been cited on at least two occasions for his pioneering work in his field.

Doctor Mancetti was Senior Staff Physician at CMP's Irvine facility and a member of the American College of Preventive Medicine. Because of his work with James, there was no reason Marvin would have any doubt concerning his credentials.

Lastly, Doctor Whetland was new to CMP. He was a member of the American Society of Clinical Oncology and according to his brief bio by CMP, he had been widely published and recognized by his peers for his successful experimental work in cancer treatments.

With the due diligence completed on the physicians, he moved to the next item on his to-do list. The task of identifying expert witnesses and medical consultants specializing in skin diseases. Although the identification process was simplified through use of the Internet, the trick required finding the right fit for this case and then conduct numerous interviews to validate the credentials and backgrounds of those he had selected.

He soon discovered there were numerous sites dedicated to expert witnesses and medical consultants and it did not take him long to generate the following list of possible candidates within California.

Dermatology Board Certified Experts--four in N. CA Bay area.
Oncology Board Certified--LA Area four, Bay Area six.
Family Practitioner Board Certified--11 S. CA.

He cut and pasted names and telephone numbers onto a work sheet to later contact each of them.

In his limited experience working as a legal investigator, Marvin had learned experts in specific fields became a very necessary part of any case. A legal firm had to be prepared to counter any claim made by an expert on behalf of their adversaries. At the end of the trial, it would be up to a judge or jury to determine which expert presented the more convincing evidence.

Now that he had completed most of the tasks Hope had asked him to do, he felt, he needed some quiet time to really put this case into perspective. He knew about James's condition and how it occurred but what still troubled him was the very perplexing Lionel Viking.

He was 100 percent sure of the doctor's dislikes of most minorities but just about anybody would trace it to his childhood upbringing. What confused him was normally most people grow beyond those dislikes as they age. Yet, he also knew some people carry the hatred to extremes until they themselves die. Yet, here is a highly educated person, a doctor, who remains focused on harming a segment of his patients. He could only keep asking himself, why? why? why? He could not understand or conclude and resigned himself by accepting, there was no clear-cut answer. Perhaps, he thought the depositions and trial would bring forth an answer.

Before he could continue his thought process, Hope entered his office.

"Marvin, now that the complaint has been received by CMP, things will begin to happen more rapidly. I am sure counsel for CMP will be Smitherson, Brunch and Fogel. They are very good lawyers and have years of experience in malpractice cases, so I expect we are going to have a very worthy competitor. What it means we will have to stay sharp and always at least one step ahead of them."

"Tomorrow, at nine o'clock, I want to meet with you and two of the staff attorneys to prepare a strategy for every facet of this case from tomorrow onward. We must assume, barring any blockbuster event, this case will go to trial and will end up going to a jury."

"Hope, you have the experience to know the legal aspects much better than I. But isn't this an open and shut case? The man is a guilty without a doubt."

"Don't make bets on it, Marvin. You have not faced high-powered lawyers who can recite the law and reference precedents set in previous cases like they personally tried each one of them. Every story has holes in it and when they get their fingers into the holes, they suddenly become gigantic chasms, which quickly swallow up all previous debate. They will fight as hard for their client as we are expected to do for James."

"Marvin the words, "preponderance of evidence" is tough to achieve and must be bullet proof. Never take any case for granted. Try everything and examine every possibility, because to win any case, you must earn it with indisputable evidence."

Marvin was in awe of Hope's fervency and her knowledge of these cases.

"Well, what can I do to give us an edge."

"I want you to think outside the box. Write yourself a long list and I mean long list of what ifs. Forget most of everything you have discovered about Doctor Viking but rather think of what you possibly could have missed."

"Now that I have brightened your day, I'll leave you with your thoughts."

Did she know what I was thinking before she came into my office, he asked himself? Is she psychic? Well, she certainly added a lot more to my things to-do list.

The next few weeks will probably be even more interesting than the previous two weeks and the enigma about Doctor Viking will continue to haunt me.

45
CHAPTER

James awoke the usual time of 6:30 in the morning and headed for the bathroom before dressing and taking his usual walk to the clubhouse for his morning workout. His cancer treatments had sapped his energy and his strength had deteriorated. This morning he just did not have the incentive or the energy to even get dressed after his bathroom visit. He had returned to bed; for even the minimal effort it took to go to the bathroom tired him.

Lately, it seemed he was always tired and although he felt less stressful, he still lacked the strength to perform his usual chores. He knew from conversation with Doctor Whetland and Marvin that his treatments were the main cause of his fatigue.

Hope had called him the previous afternoon and informed him Doctor Viking and CMP had received the formal complaint. This was the type of news he had been awaiting to hear and it raised his spirits and lowered his stress level, but the aches, pains and tired feeling did not go away.

As he lay in bed, he knew he had to call upon some inner strength to get up, get dressed and prepare to leave for his ten o'clock appointment with Doctor Whetland. Another round of therapy had been scheduled which he was now dreading. He realized it was slowly destroying whatever strength he had before the cancer took over his body. His look had become gaunt, and he appeared thinner and much older than he had one year ago.

Although the doctor had assured him, he was very happy with his progress, James felt he was not responding very well to his chemotherapy treatments and limited radiation.

Today, Doctor Whetland was to administer an advanced type of chemotherapy recently approved for use beyond the experimental trials. It would be administered locally to his right forearm and the surrounding area where the Melanoma growth was discovered and surgically removed.

Finally, he told himself he had to get up, get dressed and attempt to resume his usual activities. Somehow, he found the strength to get moving and headed to the kitchen to attempt to eat breakfast and maybe read the newspaper. He was able to eat a good portion of his favorite cereal and glance through the paper but not much more. His dire thoughts and lack of energy denied him participating in his favorite pastimes.

He realized how much time had passed, and he had to move fast to get to his appointment. He quickly placed his dish and silverware into the sink and headed for the garage, started his car and he drove to Doctor Whetland's practice in Santa Ana.

He arrived a few minutes early, parked his car and entered the reception area to sign-in and pay his ten-dollar copayment.

Within minutes, he was having his weight, temperature, blood pressure and other vitals measured and recorded. He then took a brochure on diabetes and sat on the edge of the examination table awaiting the doctor.

Doctor Whetland walked into the room and began speaking. "James you are looking a little stronger and more relaxed. All good signs your treatment is being effective. Today, as I previously informed you, I am going to change your treatment in two ways. First, I am going to eliminate the localized radiation for now which should reduce your fatigue problem. I am going to replace it with a one-time dose of chemotherapy by the name of Tumor Necrosis Factor or commonly known as TNF. It has shown great promise in both clinical studies and within the general population of patients having cancers of the extremities, very similar to your condition. Any concern or questions thus far?"

"Doctor, I am feeling a little better today, but the fatigue symptoms are with me every day. I believe the treatment is working based upon your knowledge and what you tell me, but my experience of fatigue and sleep disorders certainly contributes to my being a little depressed. I am happy you are removing me from the radiation treatments and if you believe there is a newer or improved solution without radiation, I am in favor to go forward."

"James, we knew going into this treatment process, there would be good days and bad days. Unfortunately for most patients, very little can be done to avoid side effects. Perhaps removing you from the radiation treatment will lessen your issues but I doubt if it will reduce your fatigue in the near term and you cannot expect to see any decent results rapidly, but I do know you will begin to experience improvement gradually."

"Here is what we are going to do today. First, I am going to draw a small sample of blood to have a current baseline measurement of your white and red cell count. I am happy to tell you from our previous measurements, your white cell count and red cell count have been very close to normal."

"After, I draw the blood sample, I am going to administer the TNF in a heated solution directly into the right forearm area where the growth was surgically removed. In doing so, you will feel the warmth radiate gradually within the area of application. Lastly about thirty minutes later, I will administer some additional cancer and infection fighting drugs."

"Well, I am interested in anything which may destroy the cancer, perhaps will reduce my fatigue and maybe allow me to get my strength back."

"I think it will, James but it will take time. I will also continue to administer Interferon on a scheduled basis, and I will continue to measure your total blood count and particularly your white cell count weekly for the next six weeks. I want to closely monitor how your body is responding relative to other known cases using this procedure."

"Doctor Whetland, I was just thinking about this treatment you're proposing for me. Isn't Necrosis related to death?"

"How did you know, James?"

"Crossword puzzles. I have tried to complete them for thirty years now."

"Yes, it does mean death but, in this case, we are trying to kill cancer cells, but the downside is we may also kill some healthy cells. This is one reason why I want to keep a close watch on your blood count so if too many healthy cells are being eliminated, I can administer medications to cause a positive change but only if it becomes a necessity. However, the studies I have reviewed show in 92 percent of patients, the response is very favorable."

"Doctor, let's begin and I will further study the treatment on the Internet and maybe I will learn some new crossword puzzle words."

"Okay, let's draw a vial of blood. Just a little pinch James as the needle enters your arm. Now I want you to lay flat on your back on the examination table while we preheat the solution and then we will administer it into your arm."

"Do you want another pillow? We should be done in about ten minutes, but I want you to rest for thirty minutes and then I will administer the other drugs."

"This pillow is fine and while we are waiting, I will take advantage of the time as I certainly could use a short nap, doc."

"Good idea, the nurse and I will return in about twenty-five minutes."

Doctor Whetland and the nurse administered the TNF to James and then left the room, as the procedure required a thirty-minute time lapse before administering any additional therapies.

James lay on the table with his eyes closed and thought of everything he had been through the last few months. For a reason unknown to him, although he felt lousy at times, he did feel he was winning the battle against the cancer. Time will tell he thought, but when I begin to feel better every day, I will know I am winning the battle. Now I pray this TNF stuff is the straw to break the disease cycle and then I move into the healing cycle. Before he could think any more, sleep took over and he did not awaken until the nurse and doctor reentered the room.

"All set for part two, James?"

"Yes,"

"Good, this will only take a moment or two. When we have completed giving you the medication, rest for another ten minutes. The nurse will return and let you know when it is time for you to leave."

After administering the medications, Doctor Whetland and the nurse again left the room. James lay very still but he had a wonderful smile on his face.

46
CHAPTER

A few minutes before nine a.m., the members of Hope Moran's staff directly or indirectly associated with the case, Spencer Versus Lionel Viking, M.D., were gathered into the main conference room. Hope arrived exactly two minutes before the meeting was scheduled to start. She glanced around the room to ensure everyone she had requested to attend this meeting was present before she began to speak.

"Good morning. All of you have been notified that Lionel Viking and CMP have been properly and legally served by the Superior Court with our complaint regarding our client, James Spencer. Today is day one for us and all of you here today are members of the team chosen to help our client prove his case. I expect we will be seeing quite a bit of each other for the next few months or longer. As a team, the policy of this firm for all cases is very clear and is applicable to everyone in this room."

"We do not participate in any action involving this case as individuals but rather always as a team. All communications of any sort whether it is a telephone call, email, letter, fax, or a meeting shall be well documented and shared with all members within this room. This includes all, submissions or transmissions of legal documents bound for the court or defendant's attorneys. If you meet with witnesses, opposing attorneys or anyone else relating to this case, two persons shall always attend from this team and as previously stated, these meetings shall also be well documented and shared. We cannot meet with nor fraternize with any employee, board member or others with relationships to CMP, Pac-Health, or their legal representatives except in a formal organized meeting and all present here today become aware of the meeting.

"Our opposing counsel in this action is the firm of Smitherson, Brunch and Fogel. Along established firm of very experienced attorneys, medically savvy and have been successful on several large of well-documented cases. We should never underestimate their knowledge or their tenacity. Some of you here today have observed them in a courtroom setting and understand what I am emphasizing. We also have won our share of cases and I am confident about this case, but we will have to shine a little brighter than our competition, to ensure we win this case."

"Now you have heard the preliminary ground rules, let's move on to the agenda. First action item for us is putting together a strategic plan encompassing every aspect of what will possibly occur during the entire duration of this case. So, ladies and gentlemen, let's roll up our sleeves and begin our work."

"Regarding a budget for this case, Sarah, I would like you to take the responsibility of preparing a quarterly budget for this case. Use something like Watkins versus Toddy Mining as a guide. Set up a new account with our Accounting Department and tell them the firm has taken this case on a contingency basis. All time and expenses are to be charged to the account provided from accounting. Sarah, also advise accounting to distribute a monthly report to me and a quarterly report to all team members.

"Let's now discuss discovery. Mark has more experience than most in developing discovery plans and I have already asked him to begin developing our plan. At this point, I will let Mark share with us the basics of the plan from which we will eventually operate."

"Thanks Hope," said Mark. "When you said I was to be on this case, I started to develop a plan and have already completed the basic outline. I am now ready to begin the process of prioritizing the schedule of events for discovery. From experience, I can assure all of you, for a legal firm, the Discovery Plan is the key element in any case. It becomes the basic road map for accumulating evidence to prove a case and if the evidence is strong enough, maybe the defendants facing a trial loss would be agreeable to comprise and settlement. Discovery is also the most expensive part of litigation and therefore, the plan must prioritize how this firm spends its money to ensure it gets the most bang for its buck."

"Here is what we have thus far. We have the medical record for James but beyond this evidence, the discovery process becomes a lot more complex. There is the circumstantial evidence of Doctor Viking's history of treating minority patients in a substandard manner. The circumstantial evidence of CMP transferring Doctor Viking three times after supposedly receiving reports from dissatisfied minority patients. All is this is circumstantial evidence and must be reinforced for us to be able to prove beyond the shadow of reasonable doubt.

Circumstantial evidence does not play well in court. What we need is factual evidence. Beyond this limited amount of evidence, we now possess, we need to prepare a plan for the entire range of evidence available and what could possibly be foreseen into the future. This is our challenge."

Hope said, "Thanks Mark. The Discovery Plan is our number one priority and should be completed within the next week. Mark will be meeting with many of you and will ask for your suggestions towards completing the plan."

"Now, moving on, we will require professional experts as witnesses in this case and I have asked Marvin to be responsible for this task. I know he already has a preliminary list of perspective experts. Marvin, be sure to obtain written quotations for expert fees and give them to Sarah so we can add them into the budget. Further on that note Marvin, there are three different medical disciplines, Primary Care Medicine, Oncology and Dermatology, involved in this case and we will need to look at experts from all three disciplines. You can be assured, Smitherson, Brunch and Fogel are already lining up their experts."

"Next, are depositions. I expect we can gather significant information through written interrogatories to perspective witnesses and former or current minority patients of Doctor Viking versus face-to-face meetings. It will help reduce the fees incurred. However, written deposition requests will only be used for so-called third-party witnesses who may or may not prove importance to the case unless they present significant evidence and then we dispose them. Defendants and other identified key witnesses will all be deposed here in this conference room at the appropriate time. Lastly, we will need to prepare formal legal requests for additional documents from the defendants as part of the discovery process."

"I think what I have said thus far is only a start and we should plan on a review and status meeting every Friday morning until we are confident of having a well-defined case strategy, budget, discovery plan, etc."

"Now let us switch gears and get back to evidence gathering. Mark briefly touched on this subject a few minutes ago. We should by now all become aware of most of the evidence in James's medical records and additionally what Marvin has discovered in a few places. We must now take this evidence and determine where it was found and if it is relevant. The fact that Lionel Viking's mother had strange bedfellows is circumstantial, similar too much of the other evidence we have uncovered. So, what I am suggesting, and Marvin will spearhead this process, let us continue to gather evidence but since the case has been sent to the court, let's start classifying all evidence as being factual or circumstantial. The more factual evidence, which can pass the beyond a shadow of a doubt test, builds us a stronger case.

"Look, it has been more than two hours since we started this meeting. Let us all take a fifteen-minute break, and the meeting will continue after the break."

"Marvin, before you run off, please give James a call later today and try to determine how he stands medically. Talk about his treatment and if the oncologist is giving him enough information for him to make rational decisions. Lastly, what is his demeanor? Positive or negative?"

"Good thought, Hope. I want to stay in touch with him and I'll take care of it later this afternoon. I'll drop you an email describing what I learn from my conversation with him."

The meeting resumed fifteen minutes later, and the discussion centered on the singular charge of negligence. Hope restated her conversation with Marvin regarding the subject.

"I am very confident of establishing additional charges well beyond simple negligence. There is no need to rush this along but rather be meticulous in what we do and have our evidence be beyond a shadow of a doubt. This should do it for now. See you all next Friday."

Marvin returned to his office and after checking a few telephone messages, dialed James's number. The phone was answered on the third ring.

"Hello, who is this?"

"James, it's me Marvin. Just calling to see how you are doing."

"Marvin, I am still here but I am continuing to have serious fatigue and some days I don't even feel like eating or walking or doing anything physical. Unfortunately, no one can tell me how long I must suffer this way or when this situation will end."

"I understand, James but there are something's even doctors cannot predict. Side effects from cancer treatments are one of those things. Has Doctor Whetland shared with you the treatments he is administering?"

"Yes, he has been good about spending time with me and explaining what therapies he is using and how they will affect me. Just last week, he took me off the radiation regimen and treated me with a TNF application. He said it will take up to six weeks to determine the effectiveness of this drug on my condition."

"Interesting, James as TNF is a very advanced treatment being used by Doctor Whetland. In case you were not aware, he is recognized as a leading-edge provider of advanced cancer therapies. From what I have learned about him, you are in the hands of a medical rock star."

"Wow, Marvin. I did not know he was famous, but it certainly raises my spirits."

"Good, James, it is important for you to try to stay positive. Now you have told me you are off the radiation treatments; your fatigue issue should gradually improve over the next four to five weeks. Just keep hanging in there and in time you will notice your strength slowly returning."

"I am glad to hear that good news, Marvin. How is my case progressing at the Moran firm?"

"A team has been assembled to gather evidence and do all the necessary legal chores for the case. I am sure Hope will keep you informed as things progress."

"Well, thanks for the call, Marvin. I know you are busy, and your call is appreciated. Maybe if I get some strength back, we can have a coffee together or perhaps lunch."

"I would be happy to do that, James and I do hope you begin to feel better. I know it is difficult for you now but as I said earlier, time has a way of making things better, slowly but better. I'll call you again next week to see how you are doing. Bye now."

Marvin sat for a few minutes thinking about the call and James' plight. He knew cancer treatments of any kind were difficult for all patients and

James was no exception. Currently, there just is no easy way to stop either the suffering or the disease.

He returned his thoughts to the planning meeting, and he was impressed with the professionalism of the team. We can win this thing for James he thought, but I still think there is more to this story than what we have found thus far.

47
CHAPTER

James was glad he had heard from Marvin and although he had begun to feel better, He knew he had a long way to go before he could claim victory.

It had only been one week since he had received the TNF treatment and he had visited Doctor Whetland earlier to have his blood count checked. The doctor told him his energy level would gradually increase over the next three to four weeks as the medication was eradicating the tumor.

The news brightened James' day and he now had an inner vision of being completely cured from the disease. He was very positive he was being cured.

While he had researched the disease on the Internet, he had read numerous articles of positive thinking leading to cures of many illnesses. He believed much of what he had read, and he tried hard to adapt a positive outlook in his daily life while battling the disease. He followed a regimen of breathing exercises, meditation, and easy forms of Yoga. He worked very hard to only have positive thoughts.

Two weeks later, James again saw Doctor Whetland for his continuing chemotherapy treatments and to have his blood count tested again.

Doctor Whetland looked at James and saw changes in his color, his walk and in his speech. In addition, he knew from James' blood count tests, he was healthier. This is miraculous he thought as it has only been three weeks since the TNF was administered.

He decided to question James. "James, I would like to do a short survey with you about how you feel physically now versus, four weeks ago."

"For example, let's have a sliding scale of one to ten with one being your worst and ten being your best. Please tell me how you would rate yourself physically four weeks ago?"

James contemplated a moment. "I was in so-so shape then. I would say I was a one."

"Okay, what about three weeks ago?"

"Not much better. Maybe a two or three."

"How about last week?

"Definitely better. I guess a five."

"Today?"

"Doctor, I know I am not fully healed but I will give myself a seven. I am going to win this battle."

"James, it is still too early to declare victory but maybe we are getting closer. Let me tell you why I feel this way. "The recent results of your blood tests are good and show me your body is fighting away at the disease. I noted a different person when you entered my office today with better color, more spring in your step and a more positive tone of voice.'

"James, I am sure you are feeling better, but I feel from a medical observation, you are doing great. I am thrilled about what I now see as you stand here. Something good is happening within your body and it is reflected in your physical behavior."

"Thank you, doctor. I have felt better every day for the last week or so. It is not only having more energy, but I also feel more mentally alert. I honestly believe even without medical confirmation, I have beat back the disease which wanted my life."

"James, maybe you have, and I certainly hope you have done it. Detailed tests in the next three to four weeks will confirm today's beliefs. No, champagne yet. Let it chill for another four weeks."

"See you next week, doctor when I arrive on my skateboard."

"With hope, all things are possible, James."

48
CHAPTER

Marvin spent most of the next week with a staff attorney sorting through the evidence, which had been previously gathered, and identifying it as either circumstantial or factual. Much of the evidence was factual and the staff attorneys felt they had a decent case to present should the case ever go to court.

After a review session with two of the assigned staff attorneys, Marvin returned to his office and sat at his desk for a long while. He believed they had sufficient evidence for a good case, but he was trying to think of what possibly the missing piece of information could be to have a sure thing case.

He went over the knowledge he had of Doctor Viking. I know what he did in high school, college, medical school, and CMP. What could possibly be missing? Then he saw it as clear as daylight. Residency. We know nothing about how he behaved during residency.

It must be the missing piece to fill in the time gap between college and when he started at CMP. Las Angeles County Hospital. Who do I know in LA who possibly knows someone at LA County Hospital?

Searching his address book, he found three classmates he was in contact with periodically who lived in the LA area. He placed a call to the first of his former classmates to try to find a way to obtain further information about Lionel during the time he was in residency. Unfortunately, he could not reach his classmate and from his answering machine, he quickly learned he was on vacation. He then tried to reach another friend and he was also away on a business trip. Maybe the third time I will get lucky. He dialed the number listed in his address book and within a few minutes, he was rehashing old times with another classmate who was a retina specialist in the Los Angeles area.

"Tom, Marvin Kushner. It has been a long time since we last talked."

"Marvin, glad to hear from you. How is everything?

"I am doing well and enjoy my role at the legal firm. I do some interesting medical stuff almost daily and yet no patients or the dreaded paperwork. One of the reasons I am calling you is asking if you know anybody within management at the LA County Hospital. I would like to get a little background information on a doctor who performed his residency there three years ago."

"Sorry, Marvin I personally do not know anybody.

working there but interesting enough; my partner also did his residency there a few years ago and he might know somebody who could possibly help you."

"Tom, could you do me a favor and ask your partner if he could help me. I need to find out more about this doctor regarding a legal matter."

"I would be happy to do it for you, Marvin. My partner's name is Tony Hester and if he can help then I will have him call you directly. Otherwise, I will call you and let you know that Tony cannot help you."

"Thanks, Tom. The next time I am in LA, let's plan to get together for lunch or dinner and review past and current events. It has been a while since we talked."

"Marvin, I would like to see you again, so let's make it soon. I will talk to Tony in the morning and have him call you if he can be of assistance. Thanks for the call and stay healthy."

"Thanks, Tom. I hope we can get together soon."

Wonderful thought Marvin, another piece of evidence would not hurt our case. I hope Tom's partner knows someone special.

The next morning, Marvin had finished his first cup of coffee and was starting on the second one when his telephone rang. The call was from Tony Hester.

"Tony, thank you for calling me."

"Not a problem. Marvin. Tom is a good friend and he asked me if I could help you. Please tell me what you need."

"Tony, I am doing some background checking on a doctor whose behavior is being evaluated. I would like to know if he had any questionable incidents of any kind at LA County Hospital during his residency?"

"Marvin, I have a very close acquaintance there and if you give me the doctor's name, I should be able to get you a reasonable amount of information. I would assume, all of this must remain confidential to protect everyone."

"You are correct, Tony. It must be confidential. The doctor in question name is Lionel Viking. He completed residency approximately three years ago. What I need to know is did he perform up to the hospital standards or were there any interesting issues relating to his behavior."

"Give me a couple of hours and I should be able to give you something. How useful it will be can only to be judged by you. I will call you as soon as I have something."

Thanks, Tony, I'll await your call."

Next Marvin began the chore of piecing together all the known information about Lionel. His objective was to prepare not only a story but also a profile of a doctor operating off the accepted path. He had been working almost two hours when his telephone rang again, and it was Tony Hester.

"Marvin, this may not be much but frankly what was told to me, I found rather strange. Lionel Viking was an okay doctor but in his first few months, he was openly deriding minorities. He questioned why the hospital and staff treated such patients who could not pay and who were unappreciated of the free care they were receiving."

"Sounds like Lionel, Tony."

"Wait, Marvin. It gets better. Along with his ranting about minorities, when it came time for him to examine them or to treat them, he gave them practically no time, he was arrogant and in a couple of instances he presented either a very poor diagnosis or a misdiagnosis. Other medical staff members noticed it and it was brought to the attention of the director of the residency program.

The director had a well-documented meeting with Lionel and told him very bluntly he had better get off his negative minority pulpit and start treating all patients equally. No, rushing through examinations, no insults, and no misdiagnosis. He was told if he could not adhere to the high standards expected and practiced by everyone in this hospital, then he was free to leave."

"Lionel is an interesting guy. He must have done something to change because he did complete his residency on time."

"He did apparently, and it appears it was good enough for everything to be forgiven. It is all I have to offer, and I hope it helps you."

"Tony, it is plenty and again thanks for all you did and perhaps we will get to meet whenever I get up to LA."

The news provided by Tony was more than enough evidence of the serious flaw in Doctor Viking's behavior. James was correct in saying this doctor should never practice again.

After completing the call from Tony, he called Hope to provide her the latest revelation in the ongoing Lionel Viking saga.

"Hope, I have another piece of information, which I believe now gives us a complete picture of the doctor from high school until his transfer to Fountain Valley. The missing piece of evidence was his residency."

"Hmm" murmured Hope. "We never did think about residency."

"It's okay, Hope. Here is what we now know. While in residency, he openly expressed his opinions against minorities and provides them with bogus diagnosis. He is reprimanded by the Director of Residency to get his act together or leave the program. He somehow changes his ways and finishes the program on time with no further bad marks. We now have a long trail of history about his behavior."

"Good work, Marvin."

"All the evidence we now have regarding his behavior is factual. With the preponderance of evidence, we now have, perhaps it is the beginning of the end for Doctor Lionel Viking."

49
CHAPTER

John Fletcher was Senior Medical adviser to the Chairman of CMP who had requested him to provide outside counsel with recent medical information regarding Mr. Spencer. He had conversations with all of Mr. Spencer's doctors and then placed a call to Ted Smitherson of Smitherson, Brunch and Fogel to update him on the medical status of Mr. Spencer.

"Ted, how are you today?"

"I am good, John, what can do to I help you?"

"I am calling regarding the Spencer case. In my conversations with his doctors here, it seems he is making great progress and the possibility of survival is decent."

"Thanks for the status update, John. That is good news for the patient, but Doctor Viking may not be so lucky."

"Why Ted, is there a problem?"

"John, when this case was passed to us, we were unaware of any additional wrong doings by Doctor Viking. Yet, as we got deeper into our investigation, we find there were two additional incidents of misdiagnosis by him and strangely, they were both minority patients. Because of these two cases and his subsequent treatment of Mr. Spencer, we feel there may be sufficient evidence to convict him of discrimination."

"John, I would suggest your internal legal team provide all relevant information when passing a case to us."

"Sorry Ted, I will see it gets corrected."

"Additionally, John, after a lengthy meeting with my staff attorneys assigned to this case, they felt before we go much further with this case, we might also suggest a review of Doctor Vikings past medical encounters with all minority patients. What we want to determine if this Spencer case or the others, are a coincidence or unveiling of an ongoing problem he has had, and which could grow into a gigantic nightmare for CMP."

"Wow, Ted. I guess we never connected the dots. Be assured, I will put together a medical team to review all prior minority patients of Doctor Viking and see if anything pops out of their medical records, which may represent a medical issue. I know CMP will take the appropriate action should the worst scenario become a reality."

"John, if I was in your shoes, I also would not have seen this coming. Nobody can fault CMP for the actions of an evil person, even when he is a doctor."

"Ted, I will stay in touch. Now, I must inform the board and I am sure they will take the appropriate actions needed to resolve the current and possible future issues."

"Good luck, John. I honestly hope your search is benign. In the meantime, we will put this case on hold until we hear from you. There is no sense to go on spending the corporation's money until we have a clearer picture of the Doctor. Bye for now and let's stay in touch."

John sat at his desk for a few minutes thinking about the call and he recalled Marvin's comments about CMP not needing a wayward doctor and he began to visualize negative outcomes from revisiting Doctor Viking's prior minority patients.

50
CHAPTER

After his conversation with Ted Smitherson, John immediately called the Chairman of the Board and requested if he could be available for an immediate meeting to discuss an urgent corporate matter. The chairman knew from experience of John's commitment to CMP and if he needed an immediate meeting it was for a justifiable reason. The meeting was arranged to begin in forty minutes.

While awaiting the meeting, John obtained a copy of Doctor Viking's personnel record and refreshed his memory on the two settlements and the latest incident involving James Spencer, which now was in the hands of the court.

Forty minutes later he was meeting with the chairman and discussing his conversation with outside counsel and the issues involving Doctor Viking treatment of minorities and what it could mean to CMP.

"John, the repercussions from this could be devastating for CMP and Pac Health. Here is what I suggest you do immediately. Gather two or three of our staff doctors and have them perform a detailed search of all of Doctor Viking's prior minority patients from the time he joined CMP. They are to be advised this matter is highly sensitive and it is to remain confidential. Only you are to receive details of their findings."

"I understand," replied John.

The chairman continued. "When and if any suspicious findings are uncovered, the patient is to be quickly notified and an appointment for a physical exam established. This is to be done on the pretext of a CMP "Good Health Initiative" to deter any questions from the patient why this is required. We do not want to spook our patients into thinking we have a major problem."

"Lastly, John, it is be implemented immediately and it is your only priority until we are satisfied of unearthing all probable issues. I will call an emergency meeting of the board to make them aware of the potential damage to CMP."

Within a few minutes after leaving the meeting, John was arranging special assignments for three staff physicians all of whom had long successful careers with CMP.

During the reviews of minority patient records, John's major hope was the medical team would find no catastrophic misdiagnosis provided by Doctor Viking.

51

CHAPTER

Within two hours after John received the directive given by the chairman, he was meeting with three physicians. John knew each of the doctors personally and had high regard for their medical expertise and their long-time relationship to CMP.

"Gentlemen. I have asked each of you to attend this meeting to inform you of a very serious issue facing CMP. There is a very likely possibility one of our staff doctors has been discriminating against minorities by giving false diagnosis to the patients. His name is Lionel Viking, and we currently have proof of three known patients having received false diagnosis; two of which were settled quietly prior to involving outside counsel and the third case is now in the hands of the court."

"The reason for your being here today is a decision has been made to review all of Doctor Viking's minority patient records from the time he joined CMP almost three years ago. I have already ordered all of Doctor Viking's patient records to be delivered to my office but the only ones of real interest at this time, are those of the minority patients."

"Each one of you will have to find alternatives for your daily practice without revealing the nature of your absence from the normal routine. Replacement doctors should be scheduled for at least a two-week period and if there is any difficulty finding replacements, contact me immediately."

"Obviously, all of this must remain confidential, ~~and~~ All findings are to be delivered to me daily. The review will take place in the conference room beside my office, and it is considered off limits to everyone but yourselves."

"Now, I would be happy to answer any questions?"

None of the selected doctors had questions and none of them knew Doctor Viking. But all three immediately recognized the explosiveness of the issue and the devastating effects it could have on patients and the corporation.

John assured the doctors the review would commence upon the first receipt of the requested records, more than likely tomorrow morning and beginning then they were on special assignment.

Each doctor understood the seriousness of this review and the priority for getting the reviews completed thoroughly and as rapidly as possible. Patient's lives were possibly being jeopardized.

The next morning the records began arriving to John's office and the doctors were summoned to begin the reviews. John stressed he was to be notified of any irregularities and the affected patients would be contacted accordingly. He also requested a daily summary of records reviewed along with findings and if necessary, treatment recommendations.

John had previously advised his secretary of the conference room next to his office now being off limits to all except for the three doctors. He had also told her, all details involving this situation were highly confidential and any discussion about this situation is taboo to all. She had worked for John a long time and had never seen him so tense or serious. She knew how to recognize a crisis, and this meets the crisis standard.

John and the doctors knew about HMO patient statistics in an organization such as CMP. The average primary care physician sees at least twenty patients or more per day and each patient sees the doctor approximately three times per year. Based upon these known statistics and knowing Doctor Viking had practiced at CMP for three years, he would have seen between 1800 and 2000 unique patients yearly. They then assumed about thirty percent would be minority and therefore they would normally be reviewing about six to seven hundred records just for the Irvine facility.

However, they had to consider of Doctor Viking being transferred from the LA facility to the Irvine Facility and therefore, they had to double the estimate to 1200 to 1500 records to review. They did not include his transfer to the Fountain Valley facility as it had only happened recently.

John had already advised the chairman the review had been initiated and estimated completion would be within two weeks, but until then, a daily report of relevant items would be provided. He also advised him suspect diagnosis patients would be notified to receive free physical examinations based upon CMP'S "Good Health Initiative."

At the end of the first day, just over one hundred records had been reviewed and there were only two records where the doctors felt the patients should be seen and where there was a medical issue. In both cases, the findings were deemed not life threatening for either patient.

The second day was about the same as the first day with again slightly more than one hundred records reviewed and no serious issues had been detected.

To speed up the review process, John was able to obtain a fourth doctor from another facility. Like the first three doctors, he was advised of the confidentiality of the review.

It was on the third day of review when one patient's record indicated a serious potential cardiac issue which if not treated could lead to ventricular fibrillation and possibly death. CMP notified the patient immediately with an appointment set within the next few days. The excuse used to the patient concerned a normal review of their records by a cardiologist indicated an abnormality of their cardiac function.

After reviewing almost four hundred records, the doctors concluded they would find between two and three percent of patient records with medical issues of concern.

The fourth day became the worst of the prior three days. One patient with obvious Stage 1 Hypertension, one patient with low red blood cell counts suggesting Anemia and one patient with advanced Chronic Obstructive Pulmonary Disease (COPD). The doctors recommended quick intervention for all three patients.

The seriousness of what had been found in the first four days prompted the doctors to suggest to John a complete review of all of Doctor Viking's patient records after completing the minority patient reviews. This suggestion was passed to the chairman, and he immediately agreed keeping the best interest of CMP patients in mind. The cost to perform the large-scale review and the subsequent additional medical costs were never considered in the Chairman's decision.

The review continued through days five and six with only small infractions reported by the reviewing doctors.

Day seven was more catastrophic than day four. A patient's record revealed data suggesting a serious urinary tract infection and when CMP called the patients home to set an appointment for her, they learned she had died three days before of Sepsis. The patient's name was Silvia Mercado, and she was Hispanic.

This sent fear and alarm through the doctors and management as everyone knew the cause of death was preventable if the urinary tract infection had been correctly diagnosed and if the appropriate treatment had been prescribed.

The review of the records now became urgent and two additional doctors were immediately added to the review team. The chairman personally met with the team to stress the seriousness of the situation and to these doctors, he did not have to emphasize CMP did not want any additional patients seriously sick or dying because of a misdiagnosis.

The enlarged team of doctors continued their review of the entire group of Doctor Viking's patients within four more days. Fortunately, there were only minor issues found and nothing life threatening.

In the final report, a total of twenty-seven minority patients were found to have medical issues directly related to Doctor Viking's diagnosis and the one death was also attributed to the doctor. The review of the non-minority patients showed only three improper diagnoses, which were of minor concern by the team and presented no major medical issue to the patients.

John was requested to meet with the entire CMP Board the following day after the report was completed. He presented his findings and was thanked by the board for his management of the process and quick response to the crisis.

The board requested the Director of Physicians for CMP take all the necessary steps to terminate the employment contract with Doctor Viking for cause. Additionally, he was to notify the California Board of

Medicine of the findings by CMP and to recommend the immediate suspension of Doctor Lionel Viking's license to practice medicine in the State of California.

The board also agreed the Chairman was to contact Smithson, Brunch and Fogel to begin settlement discussions with James Spencer's attorneys. He was to also to provide them details of other potential cases regarding Doctor Viking.

52
CHAPTER

When Doctor Viking returned to the Fountain Valley offices the next day, there was a message awaiting him to call the Director of Primary Care Physicians. Doctor Viking did not give it too much thought and besides, he had a patient waiting for him. He would make the call later after attending to his previously scheduled patients.

He was in good spirits and was happy to still be employed and to see all his patients. He took special time with each of them regardless of ethnicity to ensure they were satisfied with his diagnosis or prognosis. Even the nurses noted his behavior and how upbeat he was with each patient.

When he had seen all his patients scheduled to see him during his morning schedule, he returned to his office to catch up on paperwork and follow up on any messages, which needed to be answered.

He again saw the message to call the Director of Primary Care Physicians and guessed it was concerning the Spencer lawsuit. He dialed the internal number to the Director's office but there was no answer on his direct line. He therefore left a short message identifying himself and stating he would be in the Fountain Valley facility until about 3:30 p.m. if he needed to talk to him.

The afternoon scheduled appointments were like the morning and Lionel was again on his modified behavior. Greeting everyone with a smile, being very polite and he continuously reminded himself to stay focused on correctly diagnosing each patient very thoughtfully and carefully.

Later in the afternoon just before he was to leave, he received another message from the Director's office receptionist stating the Director had left for a business meeting in Northern California and the Director would be advised Doctor Viking had returned his call.

Doctor Viking left the office for the day and had planned to drive into the Angeles National Forest to do some hiking before returning to his home but the thought of the call from the Director kept popping up in his mind. He therefore decided to skip his hiking plan and drove directly to his home.

When he arrived home, there was a message on his telephone to call the Director of Primary Care Physicians at his hotel. Lionel wrote down the hotel telephone and room number but decided to wait a while before making the call.

He needed time to think as he became concerned about the reason, he would be receiving this call from the Director and why was he to call him at his hotel if it wasn't something important, perhaps it was the pending case or was it something else, he wondered.

When he gave it more thought, he had only recently been transferred and maybe the Director had only just been provided with this information of the transfer and the reason behind it plus the Spencer legal action against him.

He tried to remember the situation for which he was transferred but he had no memory of the woman or how he had treated her.

His immediate superior in Irvine had very casually dismissed it as a simple oversight and a very sensitive female patient. He was told to be careful of his joking with patients and to be more careful to test any patient suspected of any potential disease or illness to ensure they don't return with an attorney. Furthermore, he said to be exceptionally careful with seniors, patients with borderline vitals and patients exhibiting obesity and to require additional testing if there are any lingering doubts as to a healthy diagnosis.

It is now the way of the world he was told and a primary reason for high malpractice insurance rates and the soaring medical costs nationwide.

Lastly, he was then advised he would be transferred to Fountain Valley offices, as this was a corporate policy.

Although Lionel clearly resented the transfer, he understood the necessity and held no grudge against his superior in Irvine and he recognized the organization had its policy of transferring doctors when complaints were filed against them. He would be happy in Fountain Valley, and it would give him time to atone for past his behavioral misdeeds and to begin anew.

Then there was the Spencer case. He remembered James but felt he had not given him a misdiagnosis. Yes, he had a spot on his arm but to him it looked like any old age spot and after all, he had prescribed some medication to ease the itching.

By the time Lionel had gone through several scenarios regarding the Director's call, it was too late to call. I'll just have to do it tomorrow.

It can't be so important, he thought.

53
CHAPTER

Although Lionel had no memory of the Hispanic female patient, he had earlier misdiagnosed while practicing in Irvine, the patient, Elena Maria Rameriz, had no problem remembering Doctor Viking.

She had settled with CMP for five thousand dollars, but the money was of little interest to her. She was the daughter of a very successful family, had a successful husband and as a beneficiary to her parent's estate, her inheritance would make any middle-class family exceptionally happy. Her only interest in Doctor Viking was like what James desired, retribution.

She had learned of Doctor Viking's transfer to Fountain Valley and she knew she would neither see him nor be bothered by him again. Her obsession for retribution was not as focused as the one James held on too.

Fortunately, after she had seen Doctor Viking, she had been wise enough to get a second opinion and had been diagnosed in time to correct her Diabetes through prescriptive medication. She would not forget Doctor Viking's innuendos and his talking down to her. I am okay medically she thought, and he is gone but I will remember him and if our paths should cross again. I will remind him of his actions, and he will remember me for a long time.

About one month after her settlement, she was in Los Angeles helping her brother manage his chain of Mexican restaurants when she received a message to call her friend Silvia's home in Huntington Beach. She was finalizing some purchases for the restaurant, and she would return the call when she had completed all the purchases.

About one hour after receiving the message she telephoned Silvia and her friend's daughter answered the telephone.

"Elena, this is Brenda, I have some horrible news to tell you."

"Brenda, why are you crying? What is the matter?"

Sobbing, Brenda tried to talk to Elena.

"My mom died this morning. It was so sudden. We don't know what happened. She had an infection and then she was gone."

"Oh my God. Brenda I am in LA, but I will be at your house in one hour or so. I am so sorry and so sad, Brenda."

Elena spoke briefly to her brother and asked him to call her husband and inform him of the tragedy. She then

quickly went to her car for the long sad drive to Huntington Beach. She arrived at her friend's home about an hour and fifteen minutes after leaving her brother's restaurant.

She rang the bell to the house and Brenda opened the door immediately. They stood in the doorway embracing and shedding tears of remorse together before they entered the house. Silvia's husband Raul was also there to embrace her, and he also was crying.

There were other family members present, all with glum faces, handkerchiefs in their hands and most with tears in their eyes.

Elena took a seat on the couch next to Brenda and held her hand for quite a while, they were speechless. Elena was first to speak.

"Raul, please try tell me what happened."

"She wasn't feeling well the last two weeks and she had been to the doctor, and he told her it was nothing to worry about.

Just a minor infection and it would soon go away. She did not make a big fuss about it."

"Then a couple of days ago, she developed a high fever, and I immediately took her to the Emergency Room at the Fountain Valley Hospital. They quickly recognized she had a major infection and began giving her antibiotics intravenously and had her placed in the ICU section. At that point, I knew it was serious and contacted our family members."

"I met with one of her doctors later in the day and he said she had developed Sepsis and they would do everything they could to save her, but her infection was well advanced and all we could do was pray for her."

"I was there with her in ICU the entire time and there was always one or two nurses by her side monitoring her vitals and ensuring the medications were flowing. I know the hospital tried their best to save her, but she passed early this morning without ever regaining consciousness."

"I am sorry for all of you Raul and if there is anything I can do to help, just ask."

"Thanks, Elena, Silvia loved you and you were always her best friend. Please remain our friend to help our family through this terrible time."

"I will, Raul, I promise, I will."

Four hours later, Elena returned to her home and her family. She shared the news with her husband and children, and they were all sad to learn of this horrible event. The services and burial for Silvia would be held in two days. Elena told her family she would be spending considerable time at Silvia's house to help her family until after the funeral.

The funeral was held on a sunny day and was attended by more than 150 friends and relatives. There were church services reminding everyone of the special person who had passed this way and then the burial was held not far from her home. Silvia was laid to rest under a plush green carpet of grass watered with the tears from more than three hundred eyes.

On the day of the funeral, immediately after the burial, the family and friends had once again gathered at Silvia's house to reminisce and remind themselves of their good times with Silvia. They remembered all the special times together and the moments Silvia had shared with each. All agreed, she had been a wonderful wife, mother, and friend to all.

Unknown to Elena, the guests and the other family members, Brenda had received a call from CMP with a request to have her mother come in for a follow-up examination for her urinary tract infection. She sadly informed them of her mother's death.

She did not mention this call to anyone except when Elena was about to leave, Brenda told her of the strange and untimely call.

"How strange, Brenda. I did not realize Silvia was a seeing a doctor at CMP. What CMP office was calling?"

"Irvine, why do you ask?"

"Just curious as I use CMP in Irvine. I am going home now but if you need me for anything, do not hesitate to call me. I love you."

Elena left the house to drive home but she had a very uneasy feeling about CMP. All she could think of was Doctor Viking killing her best friend.

54
CHAPTER

Four days after the CMP board meeting, Ted Smitherson placed a call to Hope Moran. His call was the result of his conversation with the Chairman of CMP directing him to reach an amiable resolution of the Spencer case against Doctor Viking.

"Hope, Ted Smitherson. The purpose of my call is to determine if we can reach an out-of court settlement on the Spencer case."

"What do you have in mind, Ted?"

"Let's start with $500,000 damages. CMP would like to end this issue quickly."

"I am sure they do Ted based upon what we all now know about Doctor Viking."

"Certainly, we both know most of the story, Hope. Then let's look at it this way. James Spencer's oncologist has high expectations of a good outcome for the patient. Likely he will be among those who beat the disease after five years. The question is, what is the cost for what he went through these past few months and over the next few years?"

"Ted, we had asked for three million in our complaint and my client wants a couple of other non-monetary things."

"Tell me what they are and maybe we can satisfy his requests and reach a settlement."

"OK, first, he wants Doctor Viking terminated from CMP. Secondly, he wants Doctor Viking's license to practice medicine suspended so he can never repeat his actions against anyone ever again."

"Hope, as you know, this must be a CMP decision. Please give me about a half an hour and let me see what I can do."

"I will await your call, Ted."

Ted already knew the answer to both requests, but he was using this ploy to hopefully reduce the amount, of damages requested by Hope.

Twenty minutes later, Ted again called Hope to try and finalize a settlement.

"Hope, here is what CMP is willing to agree too. Immediate termination of Doctor Viking and notification to the state board of his discrimination actions and they will recommend to the board the suspension of Doctor Viking's medical license to practice in California. Finally, they will agree to a monetary settlement of one and one half million dollars."

"Thanks Ted, raise the monetary award to two million and I can convince my client to agree to a settlement."

"Okay, Hope. I believe I can sell those terms to CMP. Check with your client and let me know the answer."

"I'll call you back within an hour, Ted."

After her conversation with Smitherson, Hope believed James would be willing to settle as he would receive everything he asked for in the beginning of the case plus a large settlement. She then made to telephone call to James.

"James, it's me Hope. How are you?"

"Hope for whatever reason, I am beginning to feel good again. The treatments appear to be working and I am beginning to regain my strength."

"What great news James and maybe I can give you some better news!"

"They fired Doctor Viking!"

"How did you know that?"

"I didn't, it is only wishful thinking."

"Well James maybe you are psychic because Doctor Viking is in process of being terminated and maybe he will have his license to practice suspended. Is that good news for you?"

"My God, it is wonderful news. You mean CMP finally figured the bum out?"

"They did James. They absolutely did. Now do you want some more good news?"

"I am not sure I can stand so much in one day but go ahead and surprise me."

"Well CMP wants to settle the case and besides terminating Doctor Viking, they are offering a settlement of two million dollars. I told them, we could probably accept the amount but James, it is really your decision."

"Like I said a moment ago Hope, it is a lot to swallow in one day. Based upon my recent prognosis from Doctor Whetland, I am going to live at least a few more years. My main desires for retribution have been fulfilled and if they want to add a few dollars to my account. Well, that's okay with me."

"James, I will pass this along to their attorneys and I am sure we can have it completed within a week. I will call you once it is all settled."

"Hope, I want to thank you for the outstanding job you and your staff did for me. My observation is your firm was more responsible for getting Doctor Viking terminated than CMP. Again, thank you."

"You are welcome, James and I sincerely only want the best for you. Stay healthy."

Hope than called Ted Smitherson back an advised him her client was willing to accept the proposed offer. Ted thanked her and said the final settlement paperwork and check would be on her desk in four to five days.

She then called Marvin to give him the news.

"Marvin, can I disturb you with some good news.?"

"Let me guess. CMP and their counsel put forth a settlement offer for the Spencer case. Am I correct?"

"How did you know I was calling about the case?"

"You had a happy sound to your voice."

"You are partially right, Marvin. Yes, all of what you said is true and James has agreed to a two-million-dollar settlement. In addition, Doctor Viking is being terminated and may have his license to practice revoked."

"Great job, Hope. How did James accept the news?"

"With great joy and he told me he is doing good. His oncologist says he is going to live a few more years. It has been good news day for him and for us."

"Really good news but great news about James."

"Marvin, he may never realize it, but it was the result of your investigation and findings for his case which got us to where we are today. You are the true hero of this entire episode."

"Thanks, Hope, I was just trying to get justice for James and to help the firm win a case."

"I believe Ted Smitherson's firm may have also gathered damaging information about Lionel which led CMP to consider a settlement offer."

"It sounds like it was a win for James, for our firm and even for CMP."

55
CHAPTER

Elena Rameriz did not share her suspicions with anyone about the death of her friend except an attorney who had been a longtime friend of her parents and herself. He had served the entire family well with both business and personal advice over many years of a close relationship.

Two days after attending Silvia's funeral, she arranged meeting with the family attorney at his office in Los Angeles. After exchanging greetings, Elena began to speak.

"Max, I want to thank you for meeting me on short notice. I would like you to investigate the death of my friend Silvia Mercado and try to determine the name of her doctor at CMP in Irvine. I would also like you to try and find out if my friend's death was preventable."

"Elena, I know this is a very sad time for you and I promise you I will do my best to get answers for you."

"Max, for me, cost is not an issue but for my peace of mind, I and my friend's family need closure to my friend's sudden death."

Max listened to Elena's plea and understood both her desire and need for closure.

"Elena, I will begin the investigation immediately and although I have some close contacts in Orange County, it will probably take a week or more to obtain the information."

"Thank you, Max. I know you will do your best. Again, thank you for meeting with me on short notice and I look forward to hearing from you."

After Elena had left his office, Max Cohen immediately began to place a call to another attorney he had known when he taught some classes in law school and who he occasionally worked with in Orange County and who specialized in medical malpractice. His objective was to determine if he could use one of the firm's investigators for a week or so. He dialed the number and spoke briefly to the receptionist and was immediately put through to Hope Moran.

"Hi, Max. How are you?"

"I am fine, Hope and you?"

"I am great Max. What can I do for you?"

"The purpose of this call is to ask you if it would be possible to use the services of one of your investigators for a week or two. I would prefer the one you told me about who was previously a physician."

"Max, as it turns out, your timing is impeccable. We have just concluded a big case and Marvin Kushner is available and I'm sure we can loan him out to you for a couple of weeks."

"How wonderful! How can I contact him?"

"No problem, I will connect you to him in a few moments after I tell him about you."

"Thanks, Hope."

"Stay well, Max."

Hope proceeded to talk to Marvin and told him there was another attorney friend, Max Cohen, who needed an investigator for a couple of weeks. She told him, it probably involves something in the medical field since he specifically asked for you.

Marvin knew he wasn't going to be too busy with any of Hope's cases the next few weeks and told her he would be happy to do it. Moments later, Marvin was introducing himself to Max Cohen.

"Mr. Cohen, Marvin Kushner. How can I be of assistance to you?"

"Marvin, I am trying to learn about the death of a patient who was treated by CMP in Irvine. Do you know this corporation?"

"Max, I know them very well and I am afraid to ask you the name of the patient."

"Her name was Silvia Mercado."

"Max, how did she die?"

"She died of Sepsis within the last two weeks."

"Max, I am going to put you on hold for a minute or two, I have to talk to a couple of people I know."

"Marvin, I would prefer you call me back at 888 716 4455 as I have a couple of other calls to make."

"Within ten to fifteen minutes, Max."

"I'll wait to hear from you. Bye"

Marvin wasted no time getting Hope back on the telephone.

"Hope, listen to this. Max wants me to investigate the death of a woman who died from Sepsis recently. She was a patient of CMP and guess her last name."

"Marvin, I hope it was not another Lionel Viking patient.

"It was my guess, Hope. What do I do now?"

"Do what you're being paid to do. Investigate for your client and tell him the facts as you know them."

"I will confirm the name of the women with my contact first. Thanks Hope."

Marvin next called his friend John, at CMP.

"John, I am getting close to setting a luncheon date but first, I need an answer to a question."

"Okay. I'll do anything for a free lunch."

"Another legal case, Marvin?"

" Not yet but it may be in the future. Another firm in LA is asking questions and they want to know the name of a doctor who possibly mistreated a woman for a Urinary Tract Infection at CMP's Irvine office and who ended up dying suddenly of Sepsis."

"Oh well. They will find out sooner or later and we will accept responsibility. Her name was Silvia Mercado and unfortunately, she was a patient of Doctor Viking."

"John, I am sad to hear it was him. Thank you once more but maybe I hope this will put Doctor Viking away."

"I also hope so Marvin."

Marvin ended his call and then returned the call to Max Cohen.

"Max, do you have a few minutes as this story is going to take a while to tell?"

"I have plenty of time, Marvin."

"The woman who died, Silvia Mercado was misdiagnosed by a former doctor of CMP. His name is Doctor Lionel Viking. He is in process of being terminated for discrimination against African Americans and Hispanics over the course of three years. He is also a defendant in a lawsuit by a client of our firm for malpractice. In fact, he had a long history of this type of discrimination. I know because I was the one who investigated him for a case involving our client who almost died. Doctor Viking is being terminated after a long investigation by CMP, but they learned of his misdiagnosis of Mrs. Mercado too late to save her."

"CMP has petitioned the State Board of Medicine to suspend Doctor Viking's license to practice medicine in California. Max, I am sorry to give you this news because I am sure it will affect Mrs. Mercado's family and friends."

"Marvin, isn't it strange how this world we call home, works? Bad deeds happen but rarely go unpunished; for one way or another the truth finds its way out."

"The lady who requested this information was Mrs. Mercado's best friend and she is also a longtime friend of mine as I have known her almost from the time she was born. The truth will be taken very badly by her. Premature deaths, which could have been prevented, are always hard to fathom."

"I felt it would, Max. There is not much more I can say about this case now, but I would be available to assist you should this case go further."

"Marvin, I'll stay in touch with you and Hope and let you know where we go from here. Again, my thanks to you. Sadly, I now must call a friend and tell her the bad news."

56
CHAPTER

Lionel had awaked at his usual time, took his shower, shaved, and dressed in his usual work attire. He ate a small bowl of cereal, placed the dish in the dishwasher and started to leave when he remembered he left his wallet on the bedroom dresser. He retrieved his wallet and was just about to leave for the office when the telephone rang. He picked up the phone in his bedroom wondering who was calling him so early.

"Hello"

"Doctor Viking?"

"Yes."

"This is Director Stevens office from CMP. Please hold for a moment and I will notify him you are available."

Director Stevens The head of all physicians is calling me. I really must be in some kind of trouble thought Lionel.

"Doctor Viking, Doctor Stevens. Are you available to talk now?"

"Yes, I am curious about the call."

"Well," he said bruskly, "I am about to satisfy your curiosity. CMP has decided to terminate their contractual relationship with you effective immediately. You need not report to work today. All your possessions have been removed from your office and will be delivered to your home today. Your final compensation payment will also be delivered along with your belongings."

"Doctor. Stevens, I am stunned by this news. What did I do which was so wrong to precipitate this kind of action?"

"Very frankly Lionel, you deceived too many patients and from our long and costly internal investigation, you have done so for a long time and caused grief for many CMP patients. Regardless of what office you worked at while you were on the staff at CMP, you mistreated minority patients. You have disgraced this corporation and the medical profession."

"But, Doctor Stevens, I don't understand, there were only two relatively minor complaints about me."

"Are you forgetting Mr. Spencer? You may think there are only two because the other ten or so haven't caught up to you yet, but they will. Goodbye, Doctor Viking."

Before Lionel could say another word, the line had been disconnected and he stood for a while trying to digest what he had just been told.

He placed the telephone back into its holder and slowly walked into the den and dropped into the couch. He sat there stunned and could not understand what the Director had meant when he said, "the other ten or so haven't caught up to you yet."

57
CHAPTER

Elena was home in the evening with her family when she received a call from Max Cohen. It had only been one day since she had been at Max's office, and she had not expected it would be easy to get the answers she was seeking. She took his call in the den of her home, so her family would not overhear her.

"Elena, sorry to call you at this late hour but I thought it would be something you would want to know."

"It does not sound like good news, Max."

"Well, Elena, whatever news I give you is not going to bring Silvia back. Her death was unfortunate for her family and friends and unfortunately, it could have been prevented. The doctor who first saw her has an evil streak and his failure to treat her condition, eventually lead to her death."

"What was his name, Max?"

"Doctor Lionel Viking, Elena."

"Oh my God. The same doctor I had problems with at CMP. The one who misdiagnosed my diabetes."

"I am sorry about all of this, Elena. I can tell you he is being terminated by CMP for his actions against minorities. CMP also recommended to the State Board his license be suspended for his actions."

"Max, he is a murderer."

"I know, Elena but as much as we would like to repay him or harm him, we must let the legal system prevail. We know he is wrong and now we must let the law provide the retribution we seek for this man's evil actions."

"Max, I know you are right, but I hurt because I lost my best friend."

"In all my years of practice, I have never been able to understand why evil people never get to see the amount of harm they do to a wide circle of humanity."

"Tomorrow, Elena, I will contact the District Attorney in Orange County and report to him what I know about this case. I also know of others who know more than I and have offered their assistance to me to help put Doctor Viking behind bars."

"I am not sure what to say now. I should feel happy you were able to find the truth but in fact I am sad knowing this fiend killed my friend. It is hard to reconcile my feelings."

"Those feelings will remain with you for a long time, Elena, maybe until your own death. There are many things which happen to us in our lifetime which leave an impression and like a tattoo, it takes years to gradually fade away."

"Max, I did not like what I heard from you but realize you are only the messenger. I now know what happened and from this point on, it is up to you to see justice balance the scales."

"I will do my best for you."

"Max, would you handle a malpractice case for Silvia's family?

"No, it is not my field of expertise. But I can give you the name of the best attorney for this type of litigation in Orange County. A member of her staff provided me the information I have shared with you. Call me tomorrow and I will give you her name and telephone number."

"I will call you in the morning, Max and thank you for helping me. Good night."

"Good night, Elena."

The next morning Elena telephoned Max Cohen to learn the name and telephone number of the firm specializing in malpractice in Orange County.

"Good morning, Elena, my secretary will connect you to the office I am recommending. Just ask for Hope Moran and tell her Max Cohen suggested she speak with you about a case.

58
CHAPTER
PROLOGUE

Five days after his settlement discussion with Hope, James was given a check for $1,650,000 as his share of the settlement. His health continued to improve and four months after his TNF treatment, he was declared free of cancer.

Four weeks later, Doctor Viking was in the Orange County Superior Court pleading not guilty to 14 counts of discrimination against minorities and one count of manslaughter in the death of Silvia Mercado.

Seven months later, he was found guilty on all counts of discrimination and one count of manslaughter. He was later sentenced to ten to fifteen years in federal prison.

Six weeks later, Marvin Kushner was informed the California Medical Board was reinstating his license to practice medicine and CMP was offering him an executive position as Director of Medical Quality Assurance. Marvin continues to work for CMP and has been recognized by his peers for the quality programs he established at CMP.

Hope Moran successfully settled the Silvia Mercado case and is still considered the most successful medical malpractice attorney in Orange County.

www.ingramcontent.com/pod-product-compliance
Lightning Source LLC
Chambersburg PA
CBHW070356200726
48294CB00003B/935

* 9 7 8 1 9 6 1 2 5 0 7 2 7 *